FIFTH BORN

FIFTH BORN

Zelda Lockhart

ATRIA BOOKS

New York   London   Toronto   Sydney   Singapore

ATRIA BOOKS
1230 Avenue of the Americas
New York, NY 10020

Library of Congress Control Number: 2002104603

ISBN: 0-7434-1265-6

First Atria Books hardcover printing August 2002

10 9 8 7 6 5 4 3 2 1

ATRIA BOOKS is a registered trademark of Simon & Schuster, Inc.

For information regarding special discounts for bulk purchases, please contact Simon & Schuster Special Sales at 1-800-456-6798 or business@simonandschuster.com

Designed by Jaime Putorti

Printed in the U.S.A.

To my son and daughter,
whose lives inspire outrageous creativity

Acknowledgments

I'd like to thank my brother, LaVenson, for encouraging me to sing, write, and dance. Thank you to Travis for your love, patience, and support; Alex for bringing fire and passion back into my life; Leslie Bodie for your dedicated friendship and inspiration on gray winter days; Barb Dybwad for your technical talents; Susan Kemp for telling me I'm special; Susan Altenhein for being so loving; and Sylvia Delzel for being supportive and knowing I could write this book. Thank you Catherine King and Candace King for showing up in my life every time I needed you. Thank you to Dorothy Allison for letting me know I was writing fiction. Thank you to my agent, Sally Wofford Girand, for your sharp expertise; my editors, Rachel Klauber-Speiden, Tracy Sherrod, and Malaika Adero for being so profoundly good at what you do, Thank you to Demond Jarrett for lending so much time and energy to the novel. And thank you to a host of writers, artists, friends, and sweet souls who waited patiently for the birth of this novel.

FIFTH BORN

1

The Funeral

When we pulled off in the station wagon to head home to St. Louis, Granmama stood in the wake of dirt and rocks waving, her black hair blowing violently in the wind of the storm that we were leaving. I watched Granmama from the back of the station wagon until first her copper skin faded into the colors of the landscape, and then the speck that was her dress drifted, as if blown by the wind, out of the road and up the stairs of her front porch. That was the last time I saw her.

Granmama's funeral was held in the church where she had taken us on summer Sundays. The church stood tall and blinding white in the middle of a stretch of orange Mississippi dirt. Our family sat on the front pew, and because I was the baby, I sat next to Mama, holding her arm tight while my sisters and brothers sat quietly with their eyes wide open. Mama and the aunts wore veils, all their heads erect, their eyes and mouths invisible. The sun filtered through the stained-glass window, breaking the light into streams of orange and yellow where dust particles floated like dandelion seeds.

Our Grandeddy sat on the elder's pew at the front of the church. The wood dipped where he sat rocking to the soothing sound of the choir. He was the fattest black man I ever knew, and in the stained-glass light, he was so black, he was almost purple. The whites of his eyes were yellow like yolks. I stared at his face full of misery and regret for the woman that I never saw him hug or kiss. Their relationship was a lot like Mama and Deddy's, always cutting each other down with a list of regrets, but the babies came like seasons.

That day Grandeddy's face was hard and cold, not grinning behind a sip of white lightning like it usually was. In his white shirt and suspenders he looked worn, his age dusty on his black skin. I rocked with him and the rest of the family, and looked all over the church for some shift in things that would help me understand what was happening. He rolled the program tighter and tighter where the roughness of his hands against the paper sounded faint behind the harmony of the choir. Their voices lifted into the beams of the church and resonated inside my chest.

> *Walk the streets of glo-ry*
> *Let me lift my voice . . .*

The sweetness of the voices pushed Mama and the aunts into sobs and tears that sent me into tears, and I struggled to get around Mama's shaking arms and into her lap.

The adults fanned themselves to the beat, moaning like Granmama's cow when Grandeddy took her calf and sold it down the road. I watched Grandeddy.

The music paused, and the reverend stood. His voice echoed in the rafters. "He that loveth father or mother more than me is not worthy of me: and he that loveth son or daughter more than me is not worthy of me. He that loseth his life for my sake shall find it."

He wiped the spit from his mouth with a handkerchief and motioned for the choir to hum the procession song. People lined up to look in the casket, like they were lining up for communion. There we all sat waiting, me, the littlest Blackburn. The church framed us, my two sisters and two brothers, cousins, aunts, uncles, all the descendants of Grandeddy.

A tall, sturdy woman walked by in the procession and looked into my eyes. She lifted me from Mama's side, just swooped down like a hawk. When Mama looked up and saw through tears and veil that this woman was taking me to view the body, she pushed her veil up and yelled, but I cannot remember the sound that came from her mouth, because the humming had turned to singing, and somebody was shouting out the Holy Spirit in front of the casket, but when this woman looked into my eyes, the singing and moaning were muted. She looked down at Granmama and whispered in my ear, "Don't you never forget her face. You was her best granbaby. She tried to love you because she couldn't love her own."

I didn't recognize the voice that sounded so much like Granmama's, but let my three-year-old ear linger there on what felt familiar, her breath warm like comfort where nothing else made sense.

In the still of that moment I could smell Granmama's perfume, the perfume she only wore to church. She was resting in her yellow dress. The yellow dress that had yellow lace flowers over yellow satin, the dress that hung in her cedar wardrobe, the dress that she would put my hand on and say, "Flowers. Flow-ers," and I would see in my mind the tall yellow sunflowers that had grown up among the weeds behind her house. I reached for her, but her hands were gray, not brown and pink, and her face was gray and dusty. She did not reach for me, and I did not know this woman in Granmama's dress.

On the train back to St. Louis I asked Mama, "When can we go back to Granmama's?" but she stared straight ahead, moving only when the train jostled her. I let go of her arm and braced myself as I crossed the aisle. My oldest brother, Lamont, pulled me up on his lap. At nine he seemed to understand things like a grown-up. I asked, "Where Deddy?" He answered me while looking out the window, "Who cares?"

"When we goin back to Granmama house?" In the reflection I didn't see his face change, but I put my hand on his cheek to turn it to me, and felt heat rise up to his temples. Warm tears rolled over my hand, and he mumbled, "Granmama's dead." I heard the voice of my big sister Towanda, the day she ran home and said, "There was a fight after school in dead man's alley," and Mama saying, "A nigga ain't worth a damn less he's dead." I saw Granmama's gray face and yellow dress lying among broken glass and candy wrappers, muddy storm water washing over her. I leaned against Lamont's chest and cried at the window too.

I was always crying, and clinging to Mama like death would sneak up and take her away. Unlike my four older siblings, I always walked because running meant falling, and falling released blood, blood released tears, pain spewing up from some churning ulcer inside of me that nobody understood. People stopped blaming my fragile state on the fact that I was born in Mississippi one summer and was Granmama's favorite, and it hurt me more than the other kids when she died. Mama said, "She's always cried a lot."

Mama didn't seem to mind my constant tears unless we were at church or at a barbeque and one of the aunts commented, "Lord, that chile done sprung a leak again," then Mama would yank me out of the fray of flying baseballs, jump ropes, and drunk uncles, and say, "Don't be so damn sensitive, cryin over every little thing." Usually I cried softly for an additional hour, so none of the aunts would want to sit and talk to Mama, just like none of the kids wanted to play with me.

My oldest sister, Towanda, nicknamed me "cry baby-baby," because I was unlike my sisters and brothers, who had their legs planted firmly under them like young oaks with deep roots reaching beneath the asphalt. They ran up and down the streets of West St. Louis, falling and bruising without the slightest grimace. When Lamont dragged Towanda, Roscoe, and LaVern through the gangway in the red wagon, their ashy brown legs with dirty sneakers dangled. Their knees scraped against the brick of our house and the grainy tar-paper shingles of the neighbors' house—their laughter louder than the pain of scabby knees.

My mama could tell a story. Where Deddy didn't have much to say about his childhood, Mama made up for it with stories about hers. And when she told stories about something bad, she had a way of plugging a funny image in there, or throwing her head back in a big laugh with her gold tooth shining. The story about how she got that tooth was one of my favorites.

"I was in Bo's car flyin up to West Point to pick up my girl-friend. We was goin to my graduation dance, and the car caught a patch of gravel, and the next thing, my forehead was stuck in the glass of the windshield, and blood was pouring from where my real tooth used to be." That's where she laughed, loud like Grandeddy, holding on to a door frame, a chair arm, a kid's shoulder, whatever was nearest.

In the living room there is a black-and-white photo of Mama on the hi-fi. She is in a white dress, sitting in the dirt next to the car. She is posing, smiling, her dress ballooned around her. Her round face is in contrast to the white bandage that is wrapped around her forehead. Grandeddy's new car, black and chrome, is shining in the background, its front crumpled like papers. When I look at the photo, I can see the whole accident, just the way Mama describes it.

When Mama tells the story about Granmama dying, it isn't funny at all.

I sat on the front steps thigh to thigh with her. Mama watered our small lawn and hummed church songs in a low sweet voice, while Lamont, Towanda, Roscoe, and LaVern ran up and down Kennedy Avenue with the other neighborhood kids, trying to get the last bit of play in before it got too dark and Mama said come in. The smell of dry earth dampened by cool city water filled my lungs, and I sat and listened to her talk to our neighbors, who sat on their steps, watering their lawns in the same sweeping motion. Most of the grown-ups in our neighborhood had moved up from Mississippi at some point, and they always wanted to know what was happening back home.

Mama shook her head and retold the story. "Well, we were on the road coming back from down South when it happened, but Bo said Mother took one look at where he cut his self cleaning them fish and just lost her mind tryin to stop the bleeding."

I made pictures in my mind while Mama talked, trying to see Granmama running all over her house, long arms reached to grab rags, quilt squares, whatever she could to stop the bleeding. I imagined my retarded cousin Neckbone being there. He was always present when bad stuff happened, but never made it into the retelling of the story. I could hear Granmama's footsteps from the kitchen to the bathroom, and Neckbone stood at Granmama's out-of-tune piano, trying to find the notes to "Wade in the Water," his nervous, callused feet shifting from side to side on Granmama's wooden floor.

"Bo tried to tell her to calm down. He bled all over the table, but he wasn't hurting none. Lord, Lord." Mama shook her head, but kept up the steady sweeping motion with the hose.

"Mother ran to the bathroom to try to rinse and squeeze the rags, and she clutched her chest right there and had a heart attack. Bo's blood was all over the bathroom, and all over her dress. She never could stand the sight of blood."

I listened, rocking now, to music from the funeral:

What—can wash away—all my sins
Nothing—but the blood—of Jesus . . .

And I saw in my mind Grandeddy wringing the program, Granmama's obituary scraping over the crusty insides of the hands he had cut up with a fishing knife, but there were no bandages.

Death, blood, Jesus, my cousin Neckbone standing over Granmama singing "Go Tell It on the Mountain," words and images put together like puzzle pieces that made a picture of logic for Mama and the neighbors, but in my brain they swam around like tadpoles trying to find a place to settle.

2

Migrations

Mama said we were likely to tear a hole in the road as much as we went back and forth between Mississippi and St. Louis. Every summer, without fail, we took the highway south, the road thumped beneath us, and wires looped from pole to pole, landing us in a different reality, where *The Howdy Doody Show* was the only thing to watch on TV, and the sound of cicadas and crickets replaced the sound of traffic.

The summer after Granmama died, we set out for Mississippi as usual. Grandeddy sat on the porch of his store sleeping and swatting flies, waiting for the crunch of our weighted station wagon on the rock road. That year there were us five kids, Deddy, Mama, and the new baby in her belly.

I stood at Granmama's piano with my brother Lamont. He got more and more frustrated with Neckbone while trying to show him the notes. They were both ten years old. Lamont sang holding Neckbone's index finger, and pounded the keys. The two of them stood in a trance, trying to play the song right. For each note Lamont stressed a word.

Wade
In the water
Children
Wade in the water
God's gonna trouble the water

In my mind I did what Neckbone couldn't. I heard the notes and saw all of us behind the house making like the big mud hole was a big fishing hole, and I saw all the children of our family, the cousins, and my sisters and brothers being led by the march of the song into the mud. The dragonflies flew before us with their blue-and-green wings. The heat and the water disappeared us all to wherever Granmama was.

Heaven is where Towanda said she had gone. When I asked her where that was, she said, "It's not a real place, Odessa, it's like what it looked like behind her house when she was here. How she had the flowers lined up, how the corn and the sunflowers grew so tall and green even when nobody else could get corn to grow. It's just like that, but it's invisible, and she can talk to God."

Towanda sat with her thick legs hanging off Granmama's porch, and explained it to me. "Heaven is where you come from, and if you're good, where you end up. The new baby is coming from heaven, Odessa." She squinted at me to see if I was believing her.

Towanda was strong, and thick with nappy braids. She was tall for an eight-year-old, and she doled out knowledge like a grown-up. I spent a lot of time behind Granmama's house that visit, thinking that if I stared hard enough into the distance of weeds and barbed-wire fences, I would see Granmama rocking the new baby the way she had rocked me.

On the ride back to St. Louis we were only a little ways down the highway when Deddy had to stop for beer. We pulled up to the filling-station pump in a cloud of orange dirt. The station wagon jostled from side to side over rocks and potholes, and our bodies snatched to a halt. Deddy got out of the car and slammed the door all in one motion, and Mama moved half as fast, frowning, "Humph, Loni, wait a minute."

The filling station was an old weatherworn white shack with a tin Coca-Cola sign like the one that hung over Grandeddy's store. In front stood one gas pump and a rusted barrel of rainwater for washing your windows. Behind the murky window I could see the face of an old white man, glaring at Mama and Deddy on approach. His bottom lip pushed up almost to his nose, and his face sagged on both sides.

I sat in the backseat with Lamont and the Styrofoam cooler, which sat where Deddy could reach it with one hand on the steering wheel. Towanda, Roscoe, and LaVern sat in the very back of the station wagon. As soon as Mama and Deddy were inside the shack, LaVern reached over the seat and grabbed my Nakie doll that had been made from some of Granmama's old quilt squares when I was born.

Rather than taking her on, I cried and buried my head in Lamont's side. I could feel the ribs beneath his white T-shirt, and his underarms smelled like the fried onions Mama would put in her canned sardines. I tried to pull away, but he was the oldest and busy asserting himself, so his sweaty hand pulled me tight. With his other hand free he tried to snatch the doll away from LaVern.

"I know—you better give it here, LaVern, before I pull you up here by the braids!"

LaVern laughed. "Fool, you not my Deddy, with your skinny, high-yellow self."

Lamont yanked my Nakie doll, and it flew to the front seat. In LaVern's escape her foot hit the ceiling of the station wagon and cracked the plastic light cover.

Towanda and Roscoe sat behind LaVern and laughed hysterically, encouraging her to bounce up and down on the suitcases and smart-mouth, and because it was all fun now, I joined in and screamed, laughing and swatting at hands and feet.

Lamont had lost control of us. He yelled at me, rolling his eyes, "Shut up, Odessa, before I beat your ass too," then he plunged over the seat to make the others stop.

Our brawl shook the station wagon on its tires, and we didn't see Mama and Deddy coming. They opened their car doors at the same time. Mama flopped down in her seat, the passenger side dipping under the weight of her short round body. She hugged the big paper bag that I hoped had something in it for us kids. Her blue terry-cloth T-shirt was tight around her body and dark from sweat in one spot of her back. Her thick round shoulders and chubby body made the soft blue material bulge.

Deddy stood outside the open driver's side door; the sun and dust made everything look yellowed, like an old photograph. From our windows we couldn't see his face or shoulders, only the brown of his hairy muscular torso—his light blue, short-sleeved shirt unbuttoned and flapping in the dry wind. His hand wrestled with the buckle of his belt. As he pulled his belt loose, the rough, dry leather shrieked against the loops of his blue jeans, and we knew we were all going to get it. Mama crunched on her pork rinds and sighed, looking at her watch.

Deddy circled to the back of the wagon and lowered the tailgate. With the black belt wrapped around his fist, he waved Roscoe, LaVern, and Towanda out of the wagon without saying a word.

By now the old man in the gas station stood in his doorway and fiddled with the toothpick in his mouth, then wiped it on his soiled overalls. His worn face was leathery and pruned, like a dried apple. His mouth drooped at the ends, his eyes squinted closed in the same downward direction as he watched our circus.

I heard what Granmama would say: "Don't be actin a fool in front of white folks, they just waitin to justify that we ain't nothin but a bunch of heathens."

Mama crunched, with the cosmetic mirror lowered. She stared past me to the back of the car, where Deddy was now whipping Towanda, whose screeches had joined those of Roscoe and LaVern, who had already gotten it.

When Deddy opened the side door, he lifted out the Styrofoam cooler. I started to scream, new tears and sweat trailing down my round cheeks. Lamont would not be so easy; he always put up a fight. His ashy yellow legs kicked Deddy's belted fist and made him angrier.

Mama's damp arm rubbed the seat as she turned around, and the sound resonated like a fart against the plastic of the seat. Roscoe stopped moaning long enough to laugh, setting us all into the giggles again, while Lamont still kicked and Deddy grabbed. Mama glared back at us. "I'm gonna give you some-thin to laugh about." And she looked at her watch again and slapped at Deddy, who was struggling to catch Lamont's Keds. "Loni! Loni! We gotta get back on the road. We're losin time!"

Deddy fell down onto the backseat, and the fumes of beer overwhelmed the smell of Lamont's fried-onion underarm. Deddy grabbed Lamont's bare feet and dragged him across the seat. "I ain't quite done yet, Bernice."

I climbed into the back, where he had already made his rounds, and hoped that he would forget about his fifth-born.

Lamont's body knocked against the side of the car, and we sat quiet, whispering about who was going to be first when we played color cars on the highway.

Once the station wagon was rolling and Deddy was on his third beer, we fell asleep to the sound of the wind thundering in the windows.

When we got home, Deddy dropped us off and turned the sta-tion wagon around, heading back to Mississippi so he could go out behind Grandeddy's store with the other men and watch the ball games and then drive to Jackson to visit his people. Deddy and his brother Leland were the only folks from his side of the family that moved up from Mississippi.

It was obvious that Deddy and Uncle Leland were brothers, their hazel-brown eyes, their white man's pointed nose, their height. But Deddy was light-skinned and had a beer belly. At barbeques and family parties he tried to find something to say or do that would get everybody to think of him as a big shot, when he was really just our Deddy, usually drunk, or dirty from changing oil at work.

There was a dullness behind his eyes from so much wanting and not enough getting, but when nobody was looking, there was a hint of evil that reminded me of the haunted feeling I got when I looked at my dolls with their eyes open in the dark.

Leland was cool and smooth without even trying. He was brown like chocolate, and that made his teeth look perfectly white. When he smiled, popping gum, there was something clear and bright about his eyes. His clothes were pressed, without dog hair or lint.

At barbeques and family parties, he didn't say anything unless he had something to say. I watched the way the women in our family stopped whatever they were doing to listen to him—meat searing on the grill, potatoes waiting to be stirred into mayonnaise for potato salad—and so brothers-in-law often forgot to invite Uncle Leland to family parties.

When Deddy needed help doing anything, it was his big brother Leland who he called, and Leland came, ignoring the jealousy. "What you need, little brotha? I don't mind doing whatever you need, or loaning you what you don't have, because that's how family should be with one another."

Deddy seemed to need him as much as he resented him.

The evening Deddy finally came home from Mississippi, we were sitting in the living room, glued to the console watching *Gunsmoke*, when we heard him pull up. Deddy got out of the passenger side of our old station wagon, and folks we had never seen before got out too. The woman who was driving looked just like Ms. May John from church—tall, light-skinned, hair in a bun, and a duster dress that didn't look like something a skinny woman like her ought to be wearing. Out of the backseat came a woman that looked exactly the same as the driver, and then a younger woman that kind of looked like both of them, but her hair was teased into a Foxy Brown Afro. She wore an orange halter top and bell-bottom jeans. Under the streetlight they looked like a weary but serious bunch.

They all fumbled around for a while like they were trying to figure out how to get something big out of the station wagon. Finally, Deddy came up carrying a sleeping child, a little girl just my size, but yellow like him, Lamont, and these women, not brown and nappy-headed like me, Towanda, Roscoe, and LaVern.

I watched Deddy and these people and imagined myself in his arms like the little girl that he was carrying. I closed my eyes and was in the station wagon coming home from Mississippi. I felt the car slow after getting off the highway, then there was a series of stops and starts, potholes on St. Louis Avenue, but I kept my eyes closed. Then the scrambling over seats for shoes and socks, doors slamming, everybody anxious to get to the bathroom after Deddy made them hold it for the last hundred miles. In my fantasy Deddy had no choice, he had to carry me into the house, my body limp in a deep sleep.

As they got closer, I saw the straight hair and fair skin of the little girl. I could see the movement under her eyelids as Deddy marched up the stairs to the front door, and I knew that she was awake. I was curious about her, and jealous. She looked like an angel, except she smirked in her sleep.

Our coffee table, our hi-fi, and the TV console were all part of the same furniture set, wood carved in vine patterns with a background of crushed green velvet like the material of our couch, which only company was allowed to sit on. Deddy's celery green La-Z-Boy was the piece that didn't match, beer-stained and slit in one spot; masking tape slowed the continuous ripping of the worn fabric. He sat the little girl down in his chair, and the rest of us stared up at her from the floor. LaVern said, almost rolling her neck, "Who is that?" Deddy didn't answer her immediately and seemed embarrassed at our regular living room scene—the five of us huddled in front of the TV console, Mama yelling at us all the way from the kitchen, "Scoot back from the TV!"

Deddy tried to take control of the situation by standing with his thumbs hooked behind his belt, a sign we took to mean that a whipping was coming if we didn't get it together.

"Y'all act like you got some sense. This is the twins—your aints Ranell and Racine, my sistas you ain't never met. And this is my niece Devon and her daughter Gretal."

He called their names out like Santa's reindeers, and I could feel the jealousy of my sisters and brothers. Half the time he couldn't even remember our names—"That's the oldest one, yeah, light-skinned and redder than me, that gal there is the second one but she the biggest of all of them, this one here darker than all the rest of them, he my third-born, this here is the gal with long hair, look just like Bernice, and this here the baby gal, cry like a goat half the time."

Devon stood in the doorway to the living room, popping her gum to show that she was not concerned with who we were. Towanda held her head down but let her eyes look way up at Devon.

"That little girl is her daughter?"

We all knew that Devon looked like a teenager, and although I wasn't sure what was bad about that, I knew that Towanda was questioning something that wasn't supposed to be. Deddy said to his company, "Y'all come on in and rest." He motioned Devon, Ranell, and Racine to the couch. Ranell and

Racine both looked haggard, their eyes set deep in the sockets. They walked carefully over to the couch, like they were old ladies. Devon followed them, switching in her hip-hugger bell-bottoms, her boobs bouncing in that orange halter top like water balloons. We were all fixated on them, especially Roscoe, who never said much, but seemed to always be fixated on some woman's breasts. When we watched *Love American Style*, Towanda and Lamont teased Roscoe, "Why you lookin so hard, Boob Man?" But he ignored them and pressed his pelvis hard to the floor.

Deddy turned to Towanda and whispered, with his eyes bulging, "Get your smart ass up and go get them some lemonade." He picked up Gretal and sat down in his chair, putting her on his lap. At that moment I wondered where my pregnant mother was. I wanted her now, before Gretal could get to her too. I got up and ran to the kitchen where Mama was yelling at Towanda, the two of them wiping lemonade up off the linoleum floor.

"You think I go through all this trouble cleanin up this damn house for y'all to be spilling shit all over the floor. I ought to whup your ass." When Mama said those words, it was best to disappear if you hadn't already been spotted, so I went back to the living room.

Mama and Towanda came in with four cold sweating glasses of lemonade and set them down on the glass-covered coffee table. Those were the good glasses, not the plastic cups, and Mama didn't let us kids ever put anything on her table.

Gretal scooted down off Deddy's lap and took a sip and held it carefully while she climbed back up on his lap. Ranell and Racine took a sip and whispered to each other, "These glasses is oily."

Devon leaned her face on her fist in boredom and kept

popping her gum. The moment lingered on like that, us staring at them, them staring at us, and Deddy making small talk about which bus stations the twins could get off the bus on the way back.

"Don't be gettin out nowhere that's too far off the highway. Them haunkies out there are crazy. Wait till you in a town or city." Deddy scratched his head, looking for something else to say.

Eventually the twins got up and went to the bathroom to do their business together, and didn't come back until the cab blew. "Us gonna get on down the road now."

We all watched to see if Devon and Gretal were forgetting to get up, or if something drastic was about to happen—that we would be stuck with two cousins who we didn't know, and already didn't like. We all sat with our mouths open and watched the twins kiss Gretal on the cheek. A chill ran through me, and I touched my own cheek, remembering Granmama blowing on it and then kissing it.

Gretal spoke for the first time, and we all drew back at the high-pitched sound of a Mississippi drawl coming out of such a small person. "Bye, Aint Ray and Ray."

"Bye, baby. Keep an eye on your ma."

The next day, Deddy and Uncle Leland hammered and sawed in the vacant family flat over ours, and came downstairs for something to drink while Mama had Towanda and LaVern help with the dishes. Deddy offered Leland a cold one. "Michelob or Budweiser?"

"No, thanks, Loni, I just need a glass of water."

Uncle Leland sat down and grinned and winked each time

one of us girls looked at him. "Miss Towanda, Miss LaVern, and little Miss Odessa, the finest most powerful black sisters in St. Louis, Missouri. Y'all could grow up and be like the Supremes." He stood up in his boots, close-fitting jeans, and sleeveless T-shirt that showed all of his brown muscles, and started motioning a little doo-wop routine.

The three of us started laughing hysterically. Towanda tried to cover her new big teeth with the dishrag. LaVern laughed high-pitched and bobbed her head to make her long braids move, and I sat at the kitchen table, squeezed my quilt doll, and laughed so hard that the milk I had just swallowed bubbled out of my nose. Mama snatched the dishrag from Towanda and wiped my face. She smiled slightly but didn't look at Leland. "Boy, you makin these children act a fool."

Deddy sighed several times real fast, drank his beer in two gulps, and said to Leland, "Do you know Devon and that child done spent the night up there with no electricity or nothing?"

Leland finished his chuckling and smiled at Deddy. "And tell me your point, brotha."

"Don't 'brotha' and 'man' me, we got to finish." Deddy threw his bottle in the sink and stormed out the back door.

Leland turned on his way out. "That boy ain't no fun, sistas—no fun." He was still grinning, and Mama said to Towanda and LaVern in her stern voice, "Finish the damn dishes and quit grinnin."

When the dishes were done, Mama shooed LaVern and Towanda. "Go on out and play with the others, and tell Roscoe and Lamont don't be diggin in my yard." I sat right there with my doll, because I never considered Mama's command "Go play" to be for me, unless she said, "Odessa, go play."

Mama called her brother Chet and talked about Deddy's baby sister Johnell, who died in childbirth when she was twelve. "She was giving birth to Devon, and then Devon turned around and did the same thing, having Gretal when she was twelve." Mama's stories of Deddy's childhood were full of birthing tales—dead mothers, deformed or dead babies, "mongrels" from Deddy's family.

Mama said, "Chet, remember when Loni used to come to Bo's ball field to court me? He used to always have some cockeyed Blackburn cousin with him. . . . Yep, them was the days."

In my mind, Jackson, Mississippi, was a circus of ugly, bad-smelling country Blackburns, except for Uncle Leland.

I sat at the kitchen table kicking the metal legs and coloring while Mama talked to Uncle Chet. "Well, what I was callin for was to remind you about his baby sister and the daughter she had. Well, guess who Loni brought home, and didn't even ask me nothin about it? Every time he goes down South by himself, some kinda shit happens behind my back."

Mama paused for Uncle Chet's reply, which was probably something about what the Lord says about being brotherly. Mama half listened with the phone between her ear and shoulder while she cut up a chicken. I colored more quietly and quit swinging my feet so Mama wouldn't pay attention that I was listening.

She responded to Uncle Chet, "That's easy for you to say, Chet. You and Fanny don't have kids. I got plenty, and one on the way. I'm tired of doin for other folk's children. . . . I am grateful I can have kids, Chet, and that ain't the point no way." Mama had told us about little cousins who weren't even her cousins, they were just little kids who went to the schoolhouse with the Lacey kids, and didn't have anything of their own. "Some of them," Mama said, "I may as well had raised for all of the giving them handouts.

"If Loni was gonna ever start fixin up the upstairs, it was

for us to move our kids' bedrooms up there, and open it up to one house, but now them two gonna be livin better than me, and Devon ain't been in St. Louis but a week.

"Yeah, Chet, anyway, I'll pray on Sunday, but somebody around here's gonna need a better job than changin oil to help with the mortgage. He's drinkin up halfa what he make, then tryin to support somebody else's kids with the spare change. . . . Yeah, tell Fanny I said hi."

After Mama hung up, she stood back from the mutilated chicken for a minute and looked at me, suspicious. I was concentrating hard, coloring everything green. "Odessa, go tell Towanda to get in here and finish cuttin up this chicken." She wiped her hands on the dishrag and threw it in the sink like Deddy's beer bottle.

3

His Undoing

Deddy liked to fish. It's something that must have come out of the mystery of his Mississippi childhood. When he wasn't drunk, sometimes he'd get a good mind to snatch us up, grab the cooler, stop for dry ice, beer, cold cuts, and take us all to Creve Coeur Park. It would have to all happen fast before he saw something that made him mad, because then he'd leave the house and say, "Y'all don't appreciate shit. Now stay home." The door would slam behind him, and we'd know next time to go faster.

Sometimes we'd make it all the way to Creve Coeur and go swing on the swings for hours. Deddy and Mama sat in lawn chairs while he fished all day, distracted from whatever made him so agitated. When I stared at him I could see that he was content with his fishing and the ball game on the radio. I could see him as a little boy, at a pond out behind their shack in

Mississippi. Sun, june bugs, and dragonflies, nothing but a can of sardines for his lunch, for his bait, and for his dinner. He'd stay all day fishing until evening came with its cicadas and cooled the heat his skin had absorbed. Leland would come, shouting for him through the trees the way older brothers do, "Loni! Loni!" and his day of solitude would be over.

That night Deddy dropped us off and went to Leland's tavern. He came back drunk and stumbled down the hallway, using the walls to keep himself on a straightaway to the kitchen. We were used to the noises of the house while we slept. Soon would come his and Mama's argument, which led to fighting with fists and lamps. The other kids got out of bed, and I stood up in my baby bed and leaned against the wall and cried. Lamont and Towanda held on to Deddy while Roscoe and LaVern picked up the change that fell from Deddy's pockets. He swung around, laughing at Lamont and Towanda for holding on like bulldogs.

Mama ran from Deddy, to protect the new life in her belly. He stopped, laughed, and glared at her, his arms still bound by Lamont and Towanda's grip.

"Don't be tellin people you don't like who I bring home from Mississippi. My family good as yours, and I pay the goddamn bills here. If I decide to put anybody in my damn family up, it ain't none of your business!"

The tavern, the front porch, and the church were places of gossip. If you said something on the phone in your own house, you were sure to have somebody on the West Side of St. Louis tell it back to you the next day.

I tried to stay quiet in the midst of the commotion, quiet because when Deddy got drunk the sight of me in his peripheral vision made him angry. My constant tears and clinginess to babyhood, or something about where I fell in the birth line of his offspring—fifth-born, another girl—something agitated him at his very core. He turned and looked right at me.

"Bernice, you cain't even make this one shut the hell up. She about big as the rest of them and still in the damn baby bed." He stumbled over to me, and I cried in dry screams for Mama.

"I'm sick of your damn mouth now, shut the hell up!" Deddy moved out of Lamont and Towanda's grip as if he had never intended to break free until now. Mama yelled his name only one time, then doubled over in her first contraction.

In the scramble of noise and objects my baby bed was just another piece of furniture for him to throw, and make a point, for Mama not to meddle in his business. Me and my quilt doll fell like petals tossed on Granmama's grave. The mattress and the wood came crashing down, hammering me to the grates of the floor vent.

My left eye dripped blood into the darkness. I heard Mama cry, "Loni, you done gone crazy," and Deddy yelled in a cocky defense, "Stay out of my damn business and take care of the kids you got."

My sisters and brothers were quiet. The only noise was their sniffling over the debris of the baby bed, like I was dead. I waited for Mama to scoop me up, but as I drifted away all I could feel was the weight of my mattress.

Mama had false contractions that night, or maybe she knew that Deddy would stop acting a fool if he thought she was about to give birth to the son he wanted. When he found out she was pregnant, he smiled and sucked his teeth, leaning toward us kids. "That's my little nigga in there. Gone grow up and play some ball."

He had already given up on Lamont and Roscoe growing up to play for the St. Louis Cardinals. "Too many goddamn women in this family make all the boys turn into pussies."

In the morning Mama sat me on her lap on the toilet, took a piece of gauze with cool water, and wiped the dried blood off my face. She held me up to the mirror. "See? Boo-boo's all gone. Let Mama kiss it up to God."

Her wet lips felt cool where my eye still burned, and in the mirror the two of us looked like brown and fuzzy balls, like when the bathroom was steamed up from us girls taking our bath. I tried to rub my eyes to make things look clear, but Mama said, "Ah-ah-ah! You cain't rub it now. You gotta be more careful climbing out of that bed at night. You gonna worry me to death." And I saw myself doing what had never happened— climbing out of my baby bed and landing facedown on the vent in Mama's story. I let her words and her touch soothe the pain. What Deddy did was bad, but Mama nervously bounced me on her knee, calming us both until the image of me climbing out of the bed became a memory that didn't include Deddy.

We didn't go to church that morning, because Mama kept our church clothes in her closet, and Deddy was in there sleeping. She carried me on her hip into the kitchen, and I let my leg curve around to touch her pregnant belly. It was hard and tight now, and I squeezed to let the baby know that I was still the baby.

I could hardly see anything that morning. When Mama let me down, I hid under the kitchen table and listened to her make biscuits with flour, Crisco, and milk. Deddy couldn't see me under the table, but I could hear him coming. I peeked out to find Mama's legs, and with my busted eye they looked like big fuzzy brown trees. When Deddy sat down, he drank slowly. The cup only lifted and slammed back down on the table every now and then. He slid his ashy legs forward and bumped into me.

"Bernice, why you let these kids play on the floor like they ain't got no sense?" He looked under the table, and all I could make out was the narrow shape of his face and his hair, which was growing into an Afro.

"Cry baby-baby, you gone have to cut all that cryin out soon as the Loni Junior get here. You bigger than Gretal and don't see her actin a damn fool all the time." I could tell from his tone that he couldn't remember me falling out of my bed any more than I could, and I was relieved that with his headache, he couldn't see me any better than I could see him that morning.

Mama said softly, "Loni, leave her alone, she ain't feelin good this mornin."

"Hell, I'm the one with the damn headache, and all you can think about is which one a these kids is actin up rather than doin somethin useful around here." His chair rumbled against the floor as he scooted back to leave, and I unclenched my quilted doll.

Mama's face was a dark brown shadow. I could smell the life inside of her belly, her sweat gone from sharp to bland with milk that swelled inside her breasts. If she got close enough, I could tell if she was about to sing or yell. But her voice and eyes and mouth were confusing on Sunday mornings after Deddy had been drunk. She went from singing the sweet hymns that she was supposed to be singing in church to yelling at us kids, "Lamont, Towanda, Roscoe, LaVern, Odessa . . . come here right now, goddamn it!"

In church the next Sunday, Mama didn't go to the choir stand. I sat with her on the pew in front of the other kids, with Uncle Chet and Aint Fanny.

Mama asked Uncle Chet, "Did you tell Loni that I was complainin about Devon and Gretal?"

"Now you know I haven't told that no-good fool nothin."

"Well, somebody said somethin. Maybe he did that shit of giving Roscoe money to tell him what I been doin or sayin when he ain't home."

"Did he do somethin to you, Bernice?"

"Naw, we just had a argument."

"Well, what happened to Odessa's eye?" The two of them stared forward and clapped with the music while Uncle Chet waited for Mama's response. I leaned over and watched them and watched Aint Fanny sing and clap, lost in the music. Mama paused long before she answered. "I know you ain't thinkin Loni did somethin to her?"

"I just asked a question, Bernice."

"She fell out that damn baby bed."

"You need to watch your mouth in church, Bernice. What she still doin in the baby bed?"

"I guess she call herself keepin me from having this baby. But after what she did to herself, she been sleepin in the bottom bunk bed with LaVern ever since." Mama chuckled, and so did Uncle Chet. He seemed content that Mama had a response; any response would do so long as, like Towanda said, "He wouldn't have to break his daily routine and do something different."

Uncle Chet looked over and frowned at me; the lid over my left eye was still swollen. The scab was the shape of a square on the vent, and was black and crusty. "Bernice, maybe you ought to take her to the eye doctor just to make sure it didn't mess with her sight none."

The choir was singing faster and happier now. The heat of the August morning had folks passing out with the Holy Spirit. My aunts lifted up the spirits in a four-part harmony while the other choir members stomped and flailed. In my fuzzy vision the wide sleeves of their purple robes made them look like big butterflies.

Mama respected Uncle Chet's opinion, unlike that of any of her other sisters and brothers, because after he married Aint Fanny, he was the churchgoin uncle who didn't drink or dance or none of that stuff. They said he grew up to be like Granmama, a real sanctified Christian. So with Deddy's say-so—"Do what you want, but we ain't got money to spend on foolishness"—Mama took me to the eye doctors.

They dilated my pupils and took turns breathing next to my face. I tried not to breathe in their breath because Towanda said, "If you kiss a white person or breathe their breath, you will grow up and have white babies."

The doctors' words were fragmented, but by the end of a week I pieced together what they had said. "We can do these experiments on legal blindness in exchange for free eye care and glasses."

On the last day, I was fitted for frames and waited two silent hours while Mama held my hand until my new glasses came. They were warm and smelled like Windex. The nurse placed them snug on my nose, being careful not to touch me. "These are some purty frames for a cute little Negro girl."

In the mirror I stared long and hard at how the roundness of my baby face had gone and left my Granmama's high cheekbones, angular beneath my brown shiny Negro skin. My short hair was sticking out of the one-inch ponytails, and I could smell my burned, pressed hair. My right lens was thin, my left, thick.

Mama peered into the mirror, like she was trying to recognize me from some time long ago; her face was wide with being pregnant. The two of us stared at each other for a moment and saw what was familiar, and what was sharp and different.

When we stepped out onto Kings Highway, I was amazed at how clear and clean everything looked. I had forgotten how crisp the edges of things were. Mama stood with me, waiting to cross the eight lanes. Her hands clutched her purse. She had turned cold after staring at me in the mirror, and my hand dangled patiently waiting for her to see fit to hold it again.

She looked irritated, and I wondered if she was about to have another contraction. I wanted to ask her what was wrong, but I knew it might mean a sharp look, or my arm yanked. The two of us stood like separate fortresses of skin and bone. In the median I could see the distinct colors of the black-eyed Susans. They reminded me of Granmama's yard, and I remembered when I couldn't run fast enough to catch up with the other grandchildren in Mississippi, who were running in to get dinner, and Granmama lifted me up from behind and I could fly. Her legs were so long that I was already on the porch with her while the rest of them were still kicking up orange dirt. She whispered in my ear, "This my baby, because she love my greens and rutabagas."

I fantasized Granmama there on Kings Highway with me.

She lifted me over Mama, over cars, and into the passenger seat of our old station wagon; its brown interior held me safe and warm while I watched Mama, her legs landing far apart to balance the weight of the new baby. I giggled inside of myself and came back to the moment. The light was blinking Walk, and Mama was halfway to the car, her body forward but her head half turned, her gold tooth shining. "Odessa—come on!" I ran to catch up, trying not to jostle the pain behind my eyes.

Mama went to the end of August with false contractions, then the day before my first day of morning kindergarten I was worrying her to death about my hair. I begged for Mama to put my hair up in what we called a "doo-doo" ball. She kept saying, "Odessa, you don't have enough hair for that, now stop askin."

"But Gretal is wearing hers like that tomorrow."

"You ain't Gretal. Now quit worryin me to death." And she doubled over in another bout of contractions, but by now I was convinced that they occurred as a result of being worried to death.

Every morning me and Gretal walked up Kennedy Avenue with Lamont, Towanda, Roscoe, and LaVern, the six of us a herd of noise and movement, jackets, and books. Every day at noon Gretal and I waited for each other and walked home holding hands, like Mama had told us to.

Mama stayed in the hospital for two weeks, and Deddy made Cousin Devon come downstairs and watch me in the afternoon until the other kids got home. Devon was tall and beautiful. At seventeen she already had a throaty cigarette voice, and with her Mississippi drawl it made her sound like some character out of the movies.

Deddy was home eating his version of lunch—a can of Spam, leftover rice with hot sauce, and crackers. When Gretal and I came through the door, he walked out into the backyard and yelled, "Devon, get on down here so I can go back to work!" Then he said to the two of us, who stood hand in hand in the kitchen door, "Sit down and eat your rice." That's all Deddy could make, and he seemed annoyed that he had to make it, and that he had to tell two people so small to sit down and eat it.

Devon came through the back door and smacked her lips in discontent. "Uncle Loni, you gonna pay me for baby-sittin?"

"You got a roof over your head and groceries and an allowance, now I ain't gonna be lettin you make no fool out of me, girl. Do what I tell you, hear?"

Devon put her fists on her hips, rolled her neck, and marched out to the TV in the hallway. "I'm gonna call Ranell and Racine and tell them you ain't even got enough money to pay me to baby-sit."

Deddy scooted away from the table, followed her down the hall, grabbed her arm, and squeezed Devon's red cheeks between his oily fingers and kissed her hard on the lips. I looked across at Gretal, who was eating her bowl of rice like she was starved. The two of them stayed locked in a kiss. Deddy grunted with his whole mouth over Devon's lips and pressed his body on her, the same way Roscoe pressed his privates hard to the floor. I couldn't stop looking at the two of them, the muscles going limp between my legs.

Devon broke away and smiled nervously. "You crazy, Loni."

"You gonna tell Ranell and Racine what?" Deddy pinched her nipples through her sweater and grinned. Devon's tough exterior was melted now. She frowned in disappointment and flopped down on the couch in the sitting space. "Nothin."

When Deddy left, Devon emptied out her blue-jean purse that was full of mangled dolls, nail polish, nail polish remover, cigarettes, chewing gum, and a pad of paper for writing down dollar amounts from *The Price Is Right.*

She made it clear to me: "Sit down and don't ask for nothin because I ain't gettin up to get nothin."

She shouted at the TV and lifted her cigarette for puff after puff. Gretal sat on the floor next to her and teased the hair of a naked doll while she stared at the TV too. Both of them were almost white like the pictures of Deddy's mother, with black silky hair, Devon's teased into a floppy Afro and Gretal's pulled back in one long ponytail. Devon looked over at me every now and then and frowned, and Gretal acted like now she was too good to hold my hand. Instead, when Devon frowned at me, Gretal stuck out her tongue.

The closer it got to three o'clock, the more Devon looked at her watch so she could trade places with Towanda. When Towanda came in the front door, Devon clicked off the TV, grabbed Gretal, and stormed out the back door.

4

Protectors

When Mama brought the baby home, she treated me different. When I came to her with tissue now—"Mama, the booger man is in my nose again"—she just told me to blow, not to pick. When she pressed my hair now, she used her knees rather than her thighs to hold my shoulders still, and she didn't take the time to brush each piece of hair, she just yanked it through the hot comb so she could finish before Baby Benson was done with his nap. I wasn't her baby anymore, and I knew it had something to do with the eight pounds of crying, wetting, pooping Benson, but I also knew it had something to do with all the time she had to spend wondering if Deddy was going to come home drunk. In the daytime she bleached the dishes, the kitchen counter, the baby's diapers, saying, "Sometimes things don't smell right unless you kill all the germs."

For the first few days after Mama got back from the hospital, Devon stayed upstairs and waited for Deddy to come home for lunch and bring her allowance. Then she came running down the back steps and cut through the gangway to go catch the bus to the mall without even coming to pick up Gretal from downstairs. Gretal watched Devon out the girls' room window, then ran to the front to see her mama leave.

"Ma's gonna buy me a toy."

Mama huffed, "Ma's gonna cut this shit out and get a job."

One day when me and Gretal got home from school, Mama was fixing Devon's hair, getting her ready to go to the unemployment office.

"Bernice, I want to be here when Loni brings me my money. I need bus fare."

Mama yanked Devon's head back in place. "I'll give you bus fare. You need to get downtown before it gets later in the day, and when you get down to the unemployment office, talk like you got some gumption, not like some old country nigga. And go back upstairs and put on a blouse where your teats ain't hangin out. Ain't nobody gonna hire somebody who sounds ignorant and looks like a floozy."

That afternoon, Gretal and me took a nap in the girls' room. Deddy was late coming home for lunch, so Mama and Benson took a nap in her bed. Mama fell asleep first, and Gretal started running her mouth and only paused to say to me, "Shhhh—whisperrr." We tiptoed to the bathroom to play in the soap and water, and for Gretal to show me her tongue. It had cracks like dry earth. She stood on tiptoes and took down Mama's toothbrush, just reached up and grabbed one of the seven brushes without seeing whose was whose. She said, "You not supposed to just brush your teeth. You can kill extra germs if you brush your tongue."

Gretal was never afraid of saying and doing what she wanted, and I couldn't understand how she and I went to the same school yet she came home with songs and stories that were nasty, while I was happy at the discovery of "The Cow Jumped over the Moon." In the bathroom she whispered a new song for me to learn.

> My mama and your mama were sitting on a
>   bench
> My mama called your mama a big fat son-of-a-
> Pitched me out the window and landed on a
>   rock
> Along came a bumblebee and stung me on my
> Cocktails and ginger bread cost fifteen cents a
>   glass
> If you don't like it you can kiss my rusty
> Ask me no questions and I shall tell no lies
> Just follow me to my house and I'll
> Fuck you till you die.

After a while Mama woke up. "Whisper your asses back in that bed!"

After Gretal, Mama, and Benson fell asleep, I was lonely and bored. While I lay there and hoped to fall asleep, I recited, "the cat and the fiddle, the cow jumped over the moon. . . ." As I lingered just before dreams, I heard Deddy walking in Devon and Gretal's apartment, then heard him slam our kitchen door. His voice slurred, "Where the hell is everybody. Hey, Bernice!" I heard Mama stir and get up to lock her bedroom door. She mumbled, "Your drunk ass ain't comin in here waking up this baby."

Gretal lay still as a rock, her mouth wide open, snoring. Finally the house got quiet, and I imagined Deddy asleep on the sofa in the hallway. When I rolled over, Deddy was right behind me, sitting on the edge of the bed, holding the doll that Granmama had made for me. The look in his eyes was an evil coldness.

I asked carefully, "Deddy, can I have my Nakie doll?" I was afraid he was going to squeeze it till the batting came out of it.

"Shut up. You don't need this shit. Who gave you this shit?"

Even though he knew who had given me my doll, I answered, "Granmama."

Deddy was wearing the sleeveless T-shirt that I could always see sticking up from the neck of his gray service station uniform.

I rubbed my eyes and hoped he would give me my doll and go away without tearing up anything in the room. His hand came down and sealed off my whole face, airtight like Mama's canning jars. I tried to cry through the small spaces between his fingers, but instead my body screamed. The passages in my mind filled with the smell of old motor oil and beer, and the room went black, then light again, and then there were the hairs on Deddy's chest, sharp. He was clutching me close to him.

Pain throbbed in my thighs. He was hurting where I peed, shoving my Nakie doll between my legs. "You want this goddamn doll, huh? Huh?" His hand and the roughness of Nakie's stitching burned like bathwater, too hot, scalding. And I wondered in terror what he was doing to me. What if Gretal woke up and saw my pants down and Deddy with his hand between my legs? Where was Mama? Couldn't she hear the whimpering noise I was trying so hard not to make? I pulled at my panties, but his dirty hand was moving fast against his pee-pee and my bare skin. Deddy's sweat dripped onto my face and stung with stale beer. I tried to squirm from under him, but he groaned and let the weight of his body down on me, and everything was black again.

I floated there in the void between awake and sleep. I could feel my feet small and new, walking over Granmama's sandy porch. I climbed up in her lap and buried my face in her breasts, bleach and sun on her cotton dress. She put Nakie to my chest before rocking me. "Look, baby, now that's just for you. All my quilts is in here. I'm gonna be with you no matter where you is," and her voice trailed off as I watched the white puff of clouds sail past the moon, the rhythm of her chair consoling me into a deep sleep.

The light from outside the girls' room window cut across the room, and I gasped to breathe and to cry. Deddy wiped his hand on my shirt and put it over my mouth. The smell of his body was sticky mucus on my face, and my stomach convulsed, smelling him. He picked me up and turned me facedown on the bed. Gretal was still sleeping sound, her bangs matted to her forehead in sweat. He pulled the covers up over my shoulders and put his chapped lips to my earlobe: "Keep your goddamn mouth shut. You hear me? Keep your fuckin mouth shut."

I cried in my body and didn't let sound come from my mouth. I wanted to stop breathing. Instinctively I knew that I should die. That my body should curl into itself over and over until I disappeared.

I could feel Mama in the next room not stirring, her heart-beat racing trying to sleep deeper and deeper, trying not to hear. I wanted to turn my head to see if she was standing in the doorway watching Deddy and me, but I held my breath and waited for the dizziness to put me back to sleep.

When Gretal shook me, the sobering smell of coffee had filled the house, and I heard Deddy in the kitchen eating his lunch and laughing in his drunkenness. His baritone voice throbbed inside my ear. And there was my doll, Nakie, tucked tight under the covers with me; blood stained the pattern that used to be Nakie's face. I remembered the beer on Deddy's breath, his hand around my doll, ripping me with the only thing that meant Granmama to me. When I threw Nakie to the floor, Gretal yelled out, "Don't throw Nakie. I want him if you don't." I put the covers over my head and pressed my body into my own bloodstains. I hoped I'd sink past the mattress, the floor, the basement.

Gretal's voice was sharp in my ears, "You better get up, 'Dessa, Bernice made hamburgers for lunch." I squirmed back under the covers and told Gretal, "I'm sick," and let go of my tears, because if I was sick, it would be okay to cry.

Between my legs stung and I could still feel the pressure of Deddy's hand in me; my panties were cold and sticky with blood. I looked at the window and watched our turtle Chugalugs swim around in the bowl that used to hold Mama's plant cuttings. He bobbed his nose on the surface of the water, his neck stretched out like my baby finger. I watched him until breathing was easy again. I thought about winter coming, about the leaves all falling off the trees and the city going gray.

All the old trash cans in the alley wouldn't be covered by bushes anymore. I would be able to see in everybody's backyard on our street, and they would all look shabby, familiar. Sometimes if snow came and covered up the dingy sidewalks, Mama put a bucket in the backyard to catch the flakes and make real snow cones. If my throat was sore she let me have as many as I wanted.

The one sheet on the bed wasn't enough to keep me from shaking while I listened to Deddy's voice on the other side of the wall.

"Bernice, get me another beer."

"You ain't got no business drinkin like that in the middle of the day. Drink some coffee."

"You ain't got no business tryin to tell me what I need."

Then Mama's house shoes across the floor, complying.

When he went back to work, Mama came in with her homemade rum and lemon cough syrup. "Sit up and take this." She pulled the covers off, and her eyes darted around at the splotches of red that stained the sheets. Her face froze, a fork of wrinkles forming on her forehead. She bit her lip and never raised her eyes to look at me. I lay there, still shaking. My eyes begged for her to hold my stiff body. When she didn't say anything, I cried out loud, "Mama!" I called out her name over and over. Why wouldn't she touch me? Towanda said, "Don't touch the bird eggs in the backyard, because if you put your dirty hands on them, the mother will kick them out of her nest."

When she looked at me, I could tell that behind her lips she was gritting her bottom teeth against her gold tooth. I wasn't sure what she was going to do, so I looked in her eyes and started telling her what happened. "Deddy, Deddy he came in here—" But looking in her eyes, I knew she had heard, she had heard me whimpering. She had heard because when one of us groaned with a fever, she came without waiting for us to call out, she just knew to come.

"Shut up! You hear me?" Her big hand, still smelling like bleach from washing Benson's diapers, crashed down and stung my bruised thigh over and over, until everything went black again. In my dream, I was lost and could hear Granmama ask, "Where is Odessa?" I giggled and hid under the porch and waited for her to say playfully, "Maybe I'll look under the porch. Maybe she's under there." But this time I waited and waited, sisters' and brothers' sneakers passed by, and no one remembered to look for me. I was so heavy with sadness that I couldn't lift my head to call out for Mama or Deddy, who seemed so far away.

When I woke up, *Speed Racer* was on. The other kids were home from school with their backs to me, singing with the TV. I put the covers over my head to get away from the light of the TV and the smell of the full cup of homemade cough syrup still next to the bed. I was in my pajamas now and the covers were white again, my panties were clean. Benson's A & D Ointment covered the burning spots on my thighs and the place where I was torn between my legs. I must have slept through Mama cleaning me up, through Devon coming for Gretal, who was gone, and so was my Nakie doll.

Mama told my teacher, Mrs. Lawson, "She's gonna have to stay home till I can get this flu to break. I sure hope my other babies don't get it." I watched soap operas while she bleached the walls in the girls' room and scrubbed the wooden floor with Mr. Clean. Then she breast-fed Benson and bleached the dishes and cleaned the oven. She said I was a big girl now and didn't need naps anymore, so when Deddy came home for lunch, she let me watch TV in the sitting space of the hall.

He stepped over me when he came in and asked Mama, "What you got the kids home from school for?"

"Loni, Odessa's the only one home. She sick."

"Sick with what? When I was comin up, sick or not, you did what you was supposed to do, pick cotton, bale hay." He looked back down the hall at me from the kitchen table, and I was careful not to look back. Mama said, "Loni, let that chile get better. She ain't feelin good." She gave me rum and lemon cough syrup three times a day, and when it didn't hurt to walk anymore, I went back to school. I knew that Deddy couldn't remember what he had done to me, and after a while I couldn't remember either.

5

Gretal's Game

I went into first and second grade with my neck and arms growing out of my body like new tree limbs. Glasses and all, I learned to run and fall, jump double Dutch, play street ball and run-across, and my knees got scabby and dark just like the other big kids. Even though I still worked hard to put myself in the way of Mama's touch—her hand cupping her own breast for feeding Benson, her hand mashing cornmeal and canned salmon into patties—I reluctantly walked into the reality that her affection for me had shifted, like earth slipping off earth in Midwest floods.

Now Gretal was the kid who got left out of games. Nobody wanted her on their team. But the older I got, the more I liked Gretal, because she knew secrets about life that I didn't, and she was different. She talked country and was never shy about it. If somebody teased her, she didn't walk away but put her hands on her hips, rolled her neck, and cussed like she was grown—"Shut up, you bucktooth motha-fucka."

Mama and Deddy didn't whip Gretal for stuff that they would have killed us for. My other sisters and brothers hated her, because she and Devon were taking money out of our family, and thinking themselves better than us. But saying anything to them about how country they were would have meant a whipping. It wasn't easy for Lamont and Towanda to keep their mouths shut while watching Gretal do things like blow spit bubbles from between her big blood-red lips, or drool spit on knee sores, saying it was like peroxide because it bubbled. Lamont and Towanda made us laugh by making up names for Gretal. "She's the most spitty, high-yellow, country, Howdy Doody–lookin fool in our family." But Gretal kept thinking she was better than us and took to calling us black niggers. Even still, she always asked Mama, "Aint Bernice, can I come in and play?" or, "Uncle Loni, can I spend the night?"

Every time Gretal spent the night, she tried to get one of us kids to call up the spirit of Ella Mae.

"Ella Mae! Ella Mae!"

We asked Lamont what is the Ella Mae game, and he was happy to have his opportunity to scare us.

"Every kid in the Blackburn and Lacey family knows the tale. Ella Mae is the ghost of a crazy woman who drowned in Grandeddy's well after Granmama had helped deliver her born-dead baby. Everybody down in Mississippi says Ella Mae's baby died in Grandeddy's bathroom. They say that after Ella Mae was found dead in the well, her ghost could be seen in the bathroom mirror at night moaning for her baby. Her ghost has fire red skin, glowing green eyes, wild black hair, and long killer fingernails. If you go in the bathroom, shut the door, and turn off all the lights, you can look into the darkness of the mirror and call her up, Ella Mae! Ella Mae! When you see her coming, though, you had better turn on the light and get the hell out of the bathroom or she will scratch and claw you to death, and then disappear back into the dark mirror."

By then even Gretal was a little scared, but she kept asking me while Towanda, Roscoe, and LaVern kept watching TV. Gretal never got anyone to try it, but told us she'd give a demonstration. We waited in the hall and stared at the bathroom door, listening to her drawling Mississippi voice call from the bathroom, "Ella Mae! Ella Mae!" Then the light showed under the door and Gretal came out to tempt us to try it. "Y'all gotta go in there, else'n y'all never gonna see her scary face."

One night Gretal came downstairs to spend the night, and Mama and Deddy were down at Uncle Leland's tavern. So Lamont turned the bathroom light on and off until the bulb blew. He made us kids promise to say that Gretal was lying if she called the tavern to tell Mama and Deddy about the trick he was going to play on her.

As usual, Gretal asked, "Anybody want to play Ella Mae?"

Lamont said, "Yeah, but you show me again first." Gretal went into the bathroom. "Ella Mae! Ella Mae!"

Lamont held the knob with both hands, his short body strained, both feet on the frame on either side of the door, and the other four of us held his arms and waist and pulled with him.

The light switch clicked and clicked, and then Gretal started pulling the doorknob. She said nothing. The only noises were the clicking of the light switch, the sound of her sweaty palms losing their grip, and the grunts of us pulling and holding our laughter. She was silent until we heard her slam against the wall, then let loose a long screech, like the woman in The Blob. Glass broke, things were falling. The commotion was like the sound of our flat when Mama and Deddy got back from the tavern—Deddy drunk, grown bodies slamming against walls. It sounded too familiar. We all started screaming except Lamont and Towanda, who were still laughing. Now we were pulling on Lamont to let Gretal out.

"Okay, don't be crybabies." He let go of the knob and did two cartwheels into the kitchen.

We stared at the gap under the door, too scared to breathe, until the commotion stopped. The house was silent until Benson started rocking the baby bed, his stubby hands clenched around the bars. He was spitting and screaming from all the excitement. Finally the knob turned and Gretal stood in the door, and the light of the hallway drew her out of the darkness. Her permed hair was sticking up out of the ponytail, her bangs were thinner and scattered, her blouse was torn, and blood from the scratches on her face dripped red onto her white collar.

I felt sorry for her. I knew that when Devon saw the blood on the new blouse that she bought her, Gretal would get a whipping. Devon would say, "You think I'm gonna keep buying you stuff for you to mess up?"

Every time Devon whipped Gretal, we knew, because it was always on Saturday mornings after the cartoons had gone off and *Blondie* was on. They ran back and forth over the sitting space, Gretal screaming and Devon shouting, "Shut up!" The bass in her voice rumbled in the floor vent so loud that we could hardly hear the TV.

An hour later Devon would feel guilty for whipping Gretal and take her shopping. When they got back, Gretal would lean over the railing of the upstairs back porch and yell into the backyard, "Ma's gonna buy me some toys," and then, "Na-na na-na-na."

The night after Ella Mae, Gretal came back from shopping with Miss Lollipop Perfume. The bottle was shaped like an egg on a stand with the cartoon face of a beautiful blond girl with long eyelashes, wide eyes, two circles of blush, and bright red lips. The top came off and revealed a spray pump just like women's perfume. Mama was at the market, and Deddy was trying to take a nap to get ready for a party he and Mama were having that night. So Gretal wasn't allowed to come in the house, but that didn't stop her from singing her own version of the Miss Lollipop song off her back porch.

> *Miss Lollipop is not for you*
> *It's pretty and new and not for you*
> *I think you smell like poo*

Lamont said, "Ignore her, she'll stop," but she ran downstairs and cupped her hands around her eyes to squint through our back screen door, into the kitchen and down the hallway where she could see the light from the TV. She kept whispering, "Niggers—niiii-gerrrrs."

Lamont turned red and got up to chase her away, but Gretal ran off our porch and up her stairs before he could shut the door.

Deddy was still snoring, and we were all quiet until we smelled Miss Lollipop perfume. We sniffed and followed the smell into the girls' room, where on the other side of the window Gretal sat on the steps that went down from the upstairs porch, diagonally across the girls' room window, and into the backyard. She sat on the stairs with her legs hanging down, straddling one of the wooden bars. Her skirt was hiked up, her stained yellow panties pressed against the bar, her arms extended. One hand squeezed the rubber bulb to pump the bottle, and the other got the bottle as close to the window as possible.

The mist came through the screen and fell into the glass bowl where our turtle Chugalugs was floating, dead.

Gretal didn't see us, and Lamont whispered, "Let's take our chances of gettin a whuppin, let's beat her ass for all the hell she causes around here." Even though I always wanted to be with Gretal, something inside me hated her so much right then. I went with Lamont, Towanda, LaVern, and Roscoe. We barreled through the kitchen and out of the back door. Each of our five palms banged against the metal of the screen door to keep it from slamming on us, a sound that set Benson to screaming in his bed.

Towanda pushed past all of us and skipped up the stairs two by two and grabbed Gretal by the tail of her skirt, just before she got to the upstairs porch. The Miss Lollipop bottle fell and crashed in the cement of the basement hole. Towanda dragged Gretal by the arm into the backyard, where Gretal broke loose and ran. She stood in the yard chanting, "I'm gonna tell—I'm gonna tell." Her cry echoed into the house, past the bedroom where Deddy snored, and down the hallway where they met with Benson's screams.

We waited for Lamont to give the command. "Get her!"

Roscoe and LaVern went after Gretal, and Lamont and Towanda cheered them on. I went and sat on the bottom step like I was watching *Wrestling at the Chase*, because I knew we were going to get it if Deddy woke up and saw us beating up Gretal. They ran her around and around the backyard until our dog, Dog, broke loose and joined the chase. Dog was the first to catch her. He lunged and knocked Gretal into the sunken gravel driveway and licked the tears off her screaming face. Roscoe and LaVern came crashing down on Gretal and Dog.

The confusion stopped when Deddy burst out onto the porch in his sleeveless white T-shirt, which exaggerated his muscular arms, his pants still unzipped, and a belt wrapped partially around his fist.

"Line up and come past my belt! I'm gonna whup everything out here breathin!"

Lamont yelled back, "You gonna have to whup the flies too!"

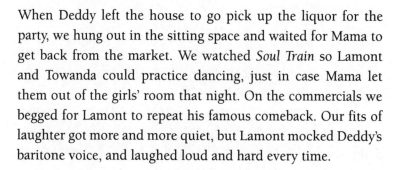

When Deddy left the house to go pick up the liquor for the party, we hung out in the sitting space and waited for Mama to get back from the market. We watched *Soul Train* so Lamont and Towanda could practice dancing, just in case Mama let them out of the girls' room that night. On the commercials we begged for Lamont to repeat his famous comeback. Our fits of laughter got more and more quiet, but Lamont mocked Deddy's baritone voice, and laughed loud and hard every time.

6

Soul Brotha

Folks from both sides of the family came to the party, and brought their favorite liquor and their favorite Chess and Motown records. They were all dressed up: the women in high heels and skintight dresses, the men in high-water slacks with their shoes shined up. Muddy Waters howled out the blues, and our house turned into a tavern. Us kids were all stuffed in the girls' room with the TV.

Gretal sat on the edge of the bed and stared at us. Lamont said, "She tryin to act like she possessed or somethin. Maybe she been touched by the curse of Ella Mae." All the kids laughed and pointed at Gretal, remembering how she called up the ghost. I put my arm around Gretal, even though she deserved their teasing for killing our turtle Chugalugs.

After *Wrestling at the Chase* came on, the attention was off Gretal, and on Dick the Bruiser and the Masked Wrestler.

When the Bruiser had the Masked Wrestler trapped in the scissors hold, me and Gretal snuck out of the room. The adults were drunk, and they paid us to do the Funky Chicken so many times that we almost fell asleep dancing, but we snapped out of it when one of the uncles pinched the wrong aunt's behind, and a fight started. The police showed up, and everybody went home. That's pretty much how all the parties they called club meetings went.

That night I overheard Mama say, "Hell, Loni, we made more money tonight than Leland probably did all weekend. From now on we doin a club meetin every Friday night. After a while we can buy our own tavern."

Uncle Leland already owned a tavern and a store. He had the most money in the family, and all the women liked his style, the way he talked like a soul brotha and dressed neat and clean, cool, like no other man I knew. Those were all the things that Deddy wanted to be. Down in Mississippi, Deddy's side of the family thought he had money because he threw it around. But while Deddy was skipping out on buying groceries and clothes for his kids, Leland was minding his own business and not trying to impress anybody. Mama said to Deddy, with her hands on her hips and her face mimicking somebody snotty, "We don't need Leland lookin down his nose at us. Hell, if it wasn't for you, he'd be some no-good nigga still down South somewhere. And if it wasn't for him hangin around Bo, he wouldn't know nothin about runnin a business." She acted like she couldn't stand Leland, but when he was talking, she melted just like the other aunts.

Except for Uncle Chet and Aint Fanny, who were too sanctified for dancing, Uncle Leland was the only family member who hadn't been invited. Towanda said, "Uncle Leland knows why Mama and Deddy don't invite him to club meetings.

Deddy's jealous, but Uncle Leland still lets them come to his tavern on Saturday nights and drink, because they're customers just like anybody else, and money is green." Leland spent his Saturday nights wiping the counter and pouring drinks for the customers who couldn't help themselves. The word he used was "alcoholic."

"When a man's got to have his drink, ain't no amount of money or nothin else gonna stand in his way, and if a brotha is gonna be givin all his hard-earned money to somebody to fill up his little milk glass all night, it just as soon be me doin the pourin as opposed to some white man. Myself, I got enough things in this world chasing after my life, I don't need liquor too."

Towanda said Deddy was an alcoholic, and that's what caused him to be looking for somebody to fight one minute, and then forget the whole thing by the next day and be laughing and trying to get Mama to pack us all up to go fishing. With Friday club meetings, Deddy had one more night a week that he was drunk, and he never seemed any closer to being a tavern owner.

Mama taught us kids, "You cain't always be lookin at who has, and who don't." But in church I heard her whisper prayers, "Lord, let Loni hurry up and make the money I know we can make. I have faith that he can do just as good as Leland. In Jesus' name, Amen."

I could feel the heaviness of her words. I opened my eyes and watched her when the whole church was whispering private prayers. I savored the last moments of seeing her without her seeing me. The congregation's prayers quieted like the wings of settling birds—then "Amen," and Mama was on guard again.

Praying and going to church was not Uncle Leland's thing. He said, "I don't need God any more than I need alcohol. Y'all go and hear that preacher preach every Sunday, and he ain't doin no better than me. He just seein the opportunity to be the man taking up the money and passin out the relief. My kingdom is at the bank."

He popped his gum, and dried another shot glass with a rag. "My kingdom come, my will be done." He winked after saying something so bad and clever.

The day after the next Friday-night club meeting, Mama did her usual routine—got up and took the station wagon full of us kids to Sulard's Farmer's Market on the south side of St. Louis. This way, she could spend her food stamps where nobody she knew would see her, and Deddy could wake up to a hot pot of coffee and work on his hangover with no kids around.

It was the first cold day of fall. Mama got out of the car, using both hands to hoist herself up. She wasn't big yet, but I could tell she was pregnant again by the way her nose flattened out, her skin got smooth, and her hair got new and wispy, not nappy around the edges. She tapped for Lamont to roll down the back window. "I'm leaving the car running so y'all can stay warm. Keep a eye on Benson, and don't come botherin me while I'm tryin to shop."

Lamont answered, "I'm fourteen, Mama, you don't have to tell me to behave."

"Fourteen ain't too old for me to whup your ass. Don't talk back when I'm talkin to you, boy."

Lamont looked forward. "Yes, ma'am." The older he and Towanda got, the more they challenged Mama. Whenever one of them talked back, my heart beat as fast as it did when Mama and Deddy were about to argue. Mama said to Towanda, "Change Benson's diaper while I'm gone," and Towanda risked rolling her eyes in response.

When Mama left, Lamont immediately taunted Roscoe, "What you lookin at, fool?"

Roscoe answered with a pitiful look on his face, "I aint lookin at you, I'm lookin out the window."

"Lookin up at women's boobs and up skirts, you little pervert."

"I ain't no pervert."

LaVern said to both of them, "We gonna all get in trouble because the two of y'all actin a fool."

Benson sat in his hooded coat being ignored. He was two now, and still wasn't potty trained. We could smell the urine in his heavy diaper right through his corduroys. He ate from a box of Cheez-Its and watched the rest of us bicker.

I said to Towanda, "Mama said change his diaper. He stinks," and she looked at me sideways.

"Odessa, I don't need you to tell me what to do. Hand me a diaper out the diaper bag, and the Wet Ones, and the Vaseline."

She pushed Benson back on the seat, "Lay down," and he jerked forward and vomited Cheez-Its all over Towanda's coat, and all over the seat. The rest of us went screaming from the station wagon, reeling from the stench. Towanda yelled, "Y'all better get back in here and help clean it up."

We were still at ages where Mama's absence sent us into an uncontrolled imbalance of mature behavior and asinine fits. We coaxed each other in and out of chaos, but there were times when no one could bring us back.

Lamont said to me, "Odessa, go tell Mama what happened. Maybe she won't get mad at you, Four Eyes." LaVern and

Roscoe stood outside the station wagon holding their noses. Lamont shooed me away. "Hurry up, girl, it's gettin cold out here."

I walked into the pavilion and looked behind me to mark where the station wagon was and what entrance I had come through. As I passed stalls of steaming hot tamales, pumpkins, apples, hot cider, I counted vendors and scanned the crowd for Mama's brown face among the mostly white faces at the market. When I got to the last stall, I stopped and looked out at the cars that were at the far end of the market parking lot. The skyline above them was smokestacks from all the factories on the Southside. Dispersed among them was a tree here and there with orange and yellow leaves. I was about to turn around and count twenty-five stalls back to the car when I spotted a car like Uncle Leland's, a brown Chevy, newly waxed, with cream-colored interior and whitewall tires. And there was Mama's green coat, and Uncle Leland's hands in her hair. When I angled myself to see beyond the glare of the windshield, I could see that they were kissing—kissing like on the soap operas. I had never seen Mama kissing Deddy. When I was very little, I remember them struggling while Deddy pushed her on the bed and shoved himself against her. I had seen Deddy kissing Devon, with his lips crammed against hers, her head against a wall with no place to go. But Leland was kissing Mama, and Mama was kissing him, slow and gentle, a dance of lips and hands.

A man shouted from a stall, "If you's not buyin, you need to move. Excuse me! Hey! Move from in front of the sausages, if you's not buyin."

I looked up at him, carrying the confusion of what I had seen. He was a fat white man with nothing but a dirty T-shirt and an apron to shield him from the cold. "If you's not buyin nothin, you's need to move."

I snapped out of it. "Yes, sir."

When I got back to the car, Lamont said, "Where's Mama?" And I lied, too embarrassed to admit what I had seen. I wanted time to ponder it before offering it up to the reasoning of my sisters and brothers. I only stuttered slightly before lying. "Ahh, she wouldn't let me tell her. She said leave her alone till she gets back to the car." We all got back in, some of us in the front, some in the very back of the wagon, and held our noses, tempered by the smell and the cold. Towanda used the whole box of Wet Ones to clean it up.

The next Saturday morning, when we got to Sulard's Market, I got on Mama's nerves, "Mama, please, can I come, please? The light bothers my eyes from sittin outside for so long."

She yelled, "No! Now get your ass back in the car," and I cried quietly, rubbing my eyes underneath my glasses, till she said, "Goddamn it, come on. You gonna drive me crazy."

When we got to the sausage stand, Mama ordered two Polish sausages, cut into thin slices for frying with eggs. She stared at the parking lot for a long time until finally she shook her head, and I pretended not to notice.

The next week I pulled the same eye stunt. I tried to make sure that kissing didn't happen, so I went under the pavilion with Mama, where the light was dimmer. Uncle Leland's car didn't show up again, and I wondered if he and Mama kissed when her and Deddy went to Uncle Leland's tavern on Saturday nights. On my way to sleep at night, I thought about it and wondered if it would be so bad if Uncle Leland became my deddy—happy and giving Mama kisses on the cheek just to see her blush.

I asked Towanda, "Have you ever seen Mama and Deddy kiss?" She answered without thinking, "No. I think they stay together because they feel like they have to. They should get a divorce, and let us kids go live in Mississippi with Mama, and Deddy can stay here."

"What's divorce?"

"Breakup, Odessa."

"If they break up, can Mama kiss somebody else if she wants to?"

"Yeah, but for one thing, Deddy ain't gonna break up with Mama without a fight, and two, if Mama ever kissed anybody, divorced or not, Deddy would show how big of a fool he can really be.

"Why you askin anyway?"

I stopped short of telling her what I had seen, because Towanda had the biggest mouth in our house. She wouldn't tell Deddy, but she would tell LaVern, and LaVern would tell Roscoe, and Roscoe would tell Deddy, if he gave him a dollar bill. So I answered her with what she would expect to hear.

"I sometimes just wish Mama was married to somebody else other than Deddy."

"Well, you old enough in the Blackburn family to know that what you wish Mama and Deddy would do, don't mean squat." I wondered then if I should just keep my mouth shut.

7

Aint Fanny's House

For Christmas, Grandeddy came up with Neckbone, and they stayed one night at each of Mama's sisters' houses, one night at Uncle Chet and Aint Fanny's house, and Christmas night at our house. Grandeddy made everybody sick going back for leftovers all evening and giving Neckbone the gristle off the turkey to chew. That night Mama had her first contraction, which meant that Grandeddy stayed in town to help out.

It was a trade-off, putting up with Neckbone's smell in exchange for Deddy impressing Grandeddy with being nice to Mama.

Deddy wrung his hands while he talked sweet to her. "Tell me what you need, Bernice, you know I'll climb a mountain for you." He then laughed nervously to see if Grandeddy was looking. "Make yourself at home, Bo, while I tend to Bernice." He bellowed commands at us kids. "Roscoe, go get your deddy and Grandeddy Bo a cold one out the refrigerator. You kids need to pick up your stuff around here. We got company. Odessa, get your Grandeddy Bo a pillow for his back."

Grandeddy got up every morning and watched the war on TV, and Deddy came in to give his viewpoint. "Sho-nuf is a mess. I tell you, if I hadn't messed up my foot in Korea, I'd be over there fightin them gooks."

"Yeah, sho is a mess . . . sho-nuf is." This was Grandeddy's first trip to St. Louis, and he sat like that, taking everything in: TV, leftover turkey, and the way his daughter and son-in-law lived. "Y'all doin better than all my folks up here. Got a big enough roof over your heads to have a great big old family, and plenty a food." He put the La-Z-Boy in the upright position and handed Towanda his plate for some more. She hid a frown from Deddy, but turned to us and made a fat face that made us giggle.

When the baby cried, Deddy got up. "Let me see if his deddy can get him to be quiet."

Fortunately, ever since Granmama died, Grandeddy didn't like going to church. So when Sunday morning rolled around, he explained, "You ain't gonna catch me in no church except for funerals and weddings. So me and Neckbone gonna be gettin on down the road, now."

As soon as they pulled off, Deddy lumbered into the bedroom, exhausted from his acting, and took a nap until it was time to get ready to go to Leland's tavern.

The next week, Uncle Chet's wife, Aint Fanny, came over almost every day and brought dinner for our family, saying, "Now stay off your feet, Bernice."

She took all of us by surprise, because up until now she acted like she was better than Uncle Chet's family, because she was from Detroit. Which really meant that when she had graduated high school in Mississippi, she could afford to catch a train a little farther north than everybody else.

We never suspected that her behavior was anything worse than weird. She came straight to the kitchen and put the pot down on the stove and went to hover over Mama and the baby, not saying much except an occasional "Amen, thank you, Jesus," when she passed Daryl in his baby bed. Mama had meaningless conversation with her about church business. Aint Fanny didn't have much to say back, just sucked her teeth and folded diapers like she was concentrating heavily on something. Mama put up with her because she was glad to have the help after Deddy pretended to help for a week.

Us kids were glad too, because it meant fewer trips to the store, which had gotten particularly grueling. We took turns and made a relay path back and forth through the snow. Grandeddy sent us for one thing, then five minutes later Deddy sent us for something else, then Mama would hear the door slam and think of something that needed to go in the stew, or pot roast or greens. Aint Fanny's sudden charity cured this temporarily.

One day she left the house, and Mama waited a long time for Baby Daryl to wake up and breast-feed, but he never did.

Mama went around the house yelling at us, "Where's the baby? Where Daryl? Towanda! Bring the baby for me to feed him."

About the same time that she realized none of us had him,

Uncle Chet walked through the door carrying Daryl wrapped in Aint Fanny's church coat. He explained, "Now calm down, Bernice, she didn't mean no harm. Lord knows she didn't mean no harm."

Aint Fanny had fixed on the fact that she and Chet never had kids. Mama said, reaching for Daryl and almost crying, "Lord, have mercy, Fanny done lost her mind."

Aint Fanny never did give up on insisting that Mama had stolen her baby. When she realized that nobody was going to let her take Daryl, she just settled on making believe that one of the older kids was hers—"The one with the long hair that looks just like Bernice." She reached right into our family like it was a basket too full of eggs and snatched my sister LaVern out.

LaVern told me about the things Aint Fanny said when the two of them went to the beauty parlor to get LaVern's hair fixed for Easter Sunday. "Now, I don't want you to want for anything, and I want you to get that old Mississippi sound out of your voice. I can't do anything about you living with the Blackburns, but you don't have to act like the rest of them."

Mama said, "Don't worry about her, she's just done lost her mind a little bit. Is it gone hurt y'all to be kind to her weakness?" It hurt any of us kids to be kind to somebody who thought we were country and ignorant.

When the church barbeque rolled around, Aint Fanny made plans to pick LaVern up, and I asked Mama, "How come I cain't go too?"

Mama glared at me, annoyed. "Nobody said you cain't go. You need to ask Fanny."

When Aint Fanny came to pick up LaVern, she looked at me like I was a lowly creature but said, "Come on, if you're coming too," and I was glad she had changed her mind. Somehow I felt like going with them would keep LaVern from getting too far from the rest of us.

When we arrived, the event was in full swing. The adults had already congregated around two tables and the barbeque pits to prepare the meal. Reverend Richards looked so different in a T-shirt and jeans that I was ashamed to look at him. It was too easy to imagine him with a beer in one hand and a spatula in the other, like one of my uncles. But this was a different party. There were no beers or half-drunk glasses of brown or clear whiskey.

LaVern and I hung close to Aint Fanny, then we both got up to join our cousins.

"Hold on, Four Eyes!" Aint Fanny was talking to me, but LaVern and I both stopped dead in our tracks, a product of being from a large passel; when one kid "gets it," all "get it." Aint Fanny shouted out, "Get back here and sit down!"

"What did I do?"

"Don't talk back to me, girl."

Aint Fanny grabbed me by the arm like I was a dirty rag and flung me onto the bench.

LaVern stared, but when Aint Fanny said to her, "It's okay, baby. You can go play," I knew that I had lost LaVern, who looked at me like I had truly done something wrong, then disappeared into the mix of cousins and other kids.

I sat on the bench all day and didn't dare contradict Aint Fanny's occasional glare by asking to go play. I looked out at the trees and sky as if I had chosen to sit down for a while and enjoy the view. I held on to my tears past the meal and the ride home, but when Aint Fanny was letting us out of the car, she called me back. "What's wrong with your hair in back? It's so nappy. And look at your clothes. I can't believe I even shamed myself with you. Go on in the house."

She reached over and snatched the car door out of my hand and slammed it shut. In the house I took comfort in the familiar smell of chili cooking for dinner. I didn't even mind the mixture of odors wafting in from the backyard—Dog's crap and freshly cut grass. Once I was safe behind the locked door of the bathroom, I let loose a quiet convulsion of sadness.

That night I made tiny braids from the bit of hair on the back of my head. Somewhere I heard that hair grows faster if you braid it. Towanda gave me some of her Dippity-Do with some advice.

"This way the braids won't just come a loose at night. Your hair don't look bad. LaVern's hair is longer than yours because she gets perms. But you gotta stop lookin so pitiful all the time, and then Aint Fanny will stop pickin on you. Act like you don't want to go with her and you don't care. Don't forget, Odessa, she's crazy, and if she wants to act like LaVern is her daughter, let her."

But I told her that LaVern acts like she's not even kin to us anymore. "She plays with Gretal more than me now, because both of them have good hair and stuff and think they're better."

When I turned four, Towanda turned ten, and when I reached the fourth grade, she had already gone to high school. She managed to keep herself out of the house and out of the way. She got straight A's and had caught up with Lamont in school. She carried the tuba in marching band because she was the strongest girl in the tenth grade. She taught the rest of us how to deal with our family.

"Listen, Odessa, Aint Fanny picks on you because she knows you're always looking for the attention, and besides, Mama's too busy keeping up with Deddy and changing diapers to notice if one less kid is begging for somethin."

To hear her talk like this always made me feel like I had no control over the things that happened in our family. There certainly didn't seem to be any sense in wondering if Mama was going to get mad at Aint Fanny, or if Mama was going to marry Leland, or if Deddy would kill both of them if he found out. It didn't seem to make any difference because the grown-ups made all the messes and us kids didn't have a choice but to come along for the ride

I realized that I couldn't let there be any more cry baby-baby. If Aint Fanny wanted LaVern, she could have her, and if Mama wanted to go into Sulard's Market and kiss all over Uncle Leland, then good, maybe Deddy would find out and they would break up, and then she would stop having babies and pay attention to the ones she had. That summer I turned ten, double digits, and started to talk back to Mama and Deddy just like Lamont and Towanda.

8

The Familiar Place

When we went to Mississippi that summer, Gretal and Devon came with us so that Deddy could take them to see Ranell and Racine. We fit in our station wagon like sardines. Even though the back of the wagon unfolded to make two rows of seats, we were now big enough that our knees touched. The sweat of three adults and six kids and the odor of urine from Daryl's heavy diapers were trapped in the car for eight hot hours, provoking agitation.

I got sick of Gretal bragging about what she was going to get. "My Aint Ray and Aint Ray gonna take me shoppin and buy me somethin for every year that I been away." LaVern begged if she could go, and without pausing, Mama said yes. I wished Aint Ray and Aint Ray would take the both of them shopping and lose them in a department store. When no one would play with Gretal, I was the one who liked her despite her spitty looks, and now she didn't even ask me to go with her. I worked hard not to cry; heat burned behind my eyes, searing my tears dry before they could roll onto my cheeks.

The day we got there, Grandeddy let Gretal bust the boil on his ankle. She had been bothering him for hours—"I'm good at bustin stuff."

She kept telling Grandeddy that she wished she was his granddaughter, but she didn't know what I knew about Grandeddy—that a grandchild was just another hand begging for candy behind the counter in his store.

"You can call me Grandeddy if you want, child. Now go on and play, Miss Flabby." Grandeddy laughed at the cleverness of the nickname for Gretal, tiny breasts and a butt more round than most nine-year-old girls. And Gretal laughed the same way her mother did when Deddy took a pinch of Devon's flesh between his rough, oily fingers.

I couldn't wait for Deddy to go see his people in Jackson so he could take Gretal and Devon to visit their own kin. Not crying about it just made me feel an itching from the inside, an irritation that hadn't found its way to the surface. When it was finally time for them to go to Jackson, I sat on the front porch with my eyes closed. Mama, Deddy, Devon, Gretal, and LaVern pulled off in the station wagon, a trail of dirt and rocks in their wake, and I remembered Granmama waving good-bye that last time, the smell of her cotton dress slipping away with the sound of the tires grinding over rocks. I stood up and put my hands in the breast of my overalls to feel where nothing had yet grown.

The other kids went down the road to our uncle's house to watch TV with Neckbone. Grandeddy was out back of Jo's house, cleaning the fish they had caught earlier that morning.

My uncle Jo and his wife were never home, but Neckbone

was the constant, loud reminder that they were someplace nearby. I didn't feel like going, so I hoisted Daryl onto my hip and went out behind Granmama's house. He could sit up now, and crawl, and at home in the playpen he could already yell nonsense while we watched TV. I sat him down in what used to be the chicken coop with a bunch of mason jar lids from Grandeddy's moonshine supplies and a wooden spoon, and let him drool and clank around in his diaper and T-shirt.

I sat on the back porch where Grandeddy now kept the old washtub, and let my mind drift away from Daryl's noise. The field behind Granmama's house was a mess. Where the flower bed used to be was now Grandeddy's broken-down truck, all rusty. It was hot back there. The sun seared everything to a dry dust. Any breeze just stirred the dirt that looked scorched. The edge of the back porch used to be lined with all kinds of colored flowers. And there used to be curtains in the kitchen window that were sheer and blew with the breeze, but Grandeddy took the curtains down a long time ago and kept the windows shut. The glass was smeared with smashed flies and fingerprints.

I remembered last summer when there were still only six of us. Mama and Deddy went to Jackson to visit his people, and we sat all night on the musty sofa waiting for something interesting to happen. Grandeddy was content to have his feet up, and to pick the disgusting catfish and mustard green dinner from his teeth. The windows were black, deep with the sound of crickets, and cows mooing way off in the distance. Finally something interesting happened.

A hornet flew in through a hole in the screen and dived at our heads. We burst into commotion. Lamont grabbed the slipper Grandeddy left behind when he shuffled into the kitchen to get the Hot-Shot bug spray. Towanda grabbed a church fan from the piano bench, and the rest of us ran from the hornet, laughing and screaming. Grandeddy came back into the room spraying. His arms seemed short, resting on his belly while he pumped the can. In only a few minutes the room was filled with bug spray and the hornet had disappeared. When Grandeddy leaned over, thinking he had found its remains, Lamont took the slipper and whacked him on the butt as hard as he could. It was silent for a moment, then we all burst into hysterical laughter.

Grandeddy made us sit on the porch for the rest of the night. Neckbone thought it was a game, so he ran back and forth past us, screaming. Until bedtime, we watched him go up the road to Uncle Jo's house and back, his grinning teeth appearing out of the black night and disappearing past slamming screen doors.

I left Daryl in the backyard. The orange dirt settled in his Afro and made his hair look red. I knew that I would get it for not watching him, but I figured that as long as everybody was watching *Howdy Doody*, and Grandeddy and Uncle Jo were drunk and busy cutting off fish heads, then I should take advantage of the fact that I had never been alone in what used to be Granmama's house. I went in the bedroom to see if anything was the same as when I was a baby. I lay across the pale green sheets that used to be bright. The covers smelled like Grandeddy's body oil, like whiskey caught up in his folds of fat. His rifle leaned in the corner where Granmama's cedar wardrobe used to be.

The wood floor was stomped up and not squared in the corners. Granmama used to say, "My baby can crawl all over this floor. Ain't no dirt on this floor. Even the corners is squared off."

I reached over and opened the nightstand drawer and pulled out a Bible that was held together with a rubber band to keep its old yellow pages from falling out. A wad of photos was crammed in between two pages. When I went to take the rubber band off, it broke.

I removed the photos. The top one was a picture of Mama as a toddler holding an apple and looking like she was about to cry. Mama had the same photo at home and showed it to company to prove how much her baby picture looked like all of ours. Mama always talks about remembering herself in that picture, all dressed up and happy until another baby tried to take her apple. For the first time I looked at that photo and did not see a baby mad about stolen fruit, but a baby whose eyes were solid black with sadness—eyes like mine that hid behind the glare of thick glasses.

On the page where the photos were crammed, there was a passage circled.

"I had many things to write, but I will not with ink and pen write unto thee: but I trust I shall shortly see thee, and we shall speak face to face." And written so neatly at the bottom of the page:

I LIVED IN FEAR SO MUCH THAT
I COULDN'T SHOW YOU ANY LOVE

I lifted the pages to my face and smelled Granmama's old perfume, and for a minute the room around me was clean again and the sheets crisp from the sun, but Daryl yelled out from the backyard and the dankness of the room was back. I ached deep inside for something clean and whole, Granmama's touch, the days when I was as new to this world as Daryl.

I stuffed the photos back in the Bible, placed it quietly back in the nightstand, and put the broken rubber band in my pocket. I planned to sneak back in Granmama's room before we went back to St. Louis and sit quietly in what felt safe, but Neckbone and my sisters and brothers made constant traffic in and out of the house, never leaving me alone again.

When we got home, I circled that passage in Mama's Bible so I could keep studying it until I knew what it meant and why Granmama liked it. Inside I could feel something that I had lost long ago trying to come back to me. A familiarity to cradle in a corner of my mind while anger and sadness brewed like a heavy storm.

9

Shelter

Our house now looked crushed and bruised in places. The walls had dents that had never been patched. Curtains that Mama made for the kitchen back before I was born were yellowing. The stain on the bathroom ceiling, from where Gretal had let the upstairs tub overflow, was getting bigger. My body and my sisters' and brothers' bodies were all getting larger as the house shrank around us. But Mama and Deddy and my aunts' and uncles' bodies just got saggier. Fewer of them danced at the club meetings. With glasses of liquor turned up to their faces, they were too drunk to cut a rug the way they used to. Some of them danced just like on *Soul Train*, like there was a camera right in front of them; the others flung themselves around the room, oblivious to their performance.

Into the early hours of morning their sounds rose to laughter, then mixed with feet stomping to music, arguments in the kitchen; one of the aunts whimpered behind the mix of noises that disappeared with slamming car doors as the sky threatened daylight.

When all the company left, I heard Mama and Deddy arguing.

"Loni, I didn't move up here to be lookin at you drunk all the time, and to be applyin for food stamps because you tryin to be Super Fly. You good a man as Leland. If your brotha can make good money up here sellin liquor rather than drinkin it all, you can too."

Deddy's speaking was slurred. "You goddamn straight I'm as good, but if you don't think so, then find another nigga who's gonna go to work every day and support more kids than the old lady in the shoe. I don't need this shit. You don't like where you livin? Get the hell out and take all these goddamn kids with you."

I sat up in bed listening, trying not to swallow too hard so I could hear if something bad was about to happen. I don't remember falling asleep, but I woke up with the sun and went looking around the house to see if there were any relatives still passed out from the club meeting.

The house was dark and musty with the smell of spilled liquor. The last album that had played on the hi-fi was still going around. The ashtrays overflowed with cigarette butts. Someone had vomited in the hallway.

I fantasized Mama finding me, putting her arms tight around me, and pulling me out of this rubble. I still wanted her attention, even though I was angry with her for having another baby, then another, and pushing me further and further into the invisible middle of the Blackburn family. It wasn't just her attention for whoever the new baby was; it was her constant tending to Deddy. When he was home, she was trying to talk and laugh around his alcoholic moods, and when he wasn't, she was busy on the phone talking about what she was going to do to put an end to it.

If she was talking to one of the aunts, she was going to help him get it figured out, like how all the aunts stayed married to their husbands. If she was talking to one of our neighbors, she was going to do better for herself and for us.

For all of us, there was confusion in either seeing Mama standing in the mirror to look good for Deddy, or seeing her gather up our stuff to run away from him. Even still, there was a coldness from Mama that seemed especially for me, especially for the secrets we harbored.

I stood in the middle of the hallway that morning hearing every funeral song that had ever been wailed out into the ceiling of our church, and I wanted Granmama, her words, the things I never got to know of her.

My mind was about to fly into memories, all played out in the place where I stood, when Mama staggered out of the bedroom and into the kitchen to start coffee for her and Deddy. She sat down with her back to the sitting space. That day, she held the frozen water bottle to the back of her head, to keep down the swelling of whatever happened after I fell asleep. When I came into the kitchen, she got up and put the water bottle back in the freezer and went over to the stove.

"Good mornin, Mama," I mumbled quietly, not knowing if I wanted to hug her or run away out the back door, down the alley as far as I could run past the corner store, the school, until I got to something that I didn't recognize.

"Good mornin." Her voice was hoarse.

I couldn't look at her because her hair and face looked worn like the walls around us. Without speaking or looking at each other, the two of us made breakfast. I was glad to be in her company like when I was little. While we were cooking, Mama picked up the phone and called Leland.

"I sure wish you would come over here and talk to him. I don't want him to wake up and start actin a fool again."

She didn't tell Leland that her and Deddy had been fighting about him. Mama rolled out the biscuits while she talked, and my heart pounded in my ears as I listened for the squeak of the bedroom door. If Deddy woke up now, he would kill her for calling Leland for help.

When Leland came by, he gave me and LaVern and Benson and Daryl each a turn being picked up in his arms, and talked to each of us about school or something special. I felt much better after he got there. The house didn't seem so dirty anymore, and my sadness and frustration lifted.

LaVern tried to tell him in her new proper voice, "I don't want you picking me up, I'm too big for that."

But Leland waited till she wasn't looking and scooped her up anyway. "Somebody needs to put your hair back in pigtails and beat the britches offa you, girl. The more high and mighty you are, the harder you fall."

Her eyes rolled and stayed closed until Leland shook his head and put her down.

"You ain't my deddy."

Mama just looked at her sideways as LaVern stormed down the hallway.

When Leland picked me up, he looked me straight in the eyes, right through my thick glasses, and said, "How's my baby gal? Sweet as sugar and brown as molasses." He pulled a piece of gum from behind my ear, then put me down and said, "Get your shoes on."

Because Leland never got invited to family gatherings, we didn't know him very well, except for listening to him talk about the way folks are in their nature, and listening to Mama and Deddy talk about him after coming back from free drinks at his tavern on Saturday night. But, Mama had asked for his help, and I was glad, because she had never asked for anybody's help until now.

Deddy was still asleep, so Leland saw Mama and us to the door. "Y'all go on. I'll talk to Loni."

Lamont and Towanda went off down the street without the rest of us, without even turning around to say where they were going. Mama started to yell after them but realized that they were already gone and there was nothing she could do about it. She turned to Leland and smiled. "I'm gonna go on and do my shoppin."

Leland looked down the street at Lamont and Towanda and popped his gum with a concerned look on his face. He smoothed his mustache with one hand and said, "Leave them alone, they old enough to take care of themselves, but somethin gonna have to be worked out here. You got five more babies to do better for, girl. You didn't get away from Mississippi to have a bunch of miserable kids and be gettin the hell beat out of you every week. I never planned on sayin or doin nothin unless you asked for it, Bernice, but now you done asked. I'm tellin you, you know you can do better for a man than the one you got."

When we got in the car, Mama turned the key hard in the ignition, and to keep LaVern and Roscoe from suspecting that Leland was the man she wanted, she whipped the station wagon out of the parking space and said, "Leland think he better than everybody else."

We went to Sulard's Market, and this time I stayed in the station wagon while she went in to shop. She left the heat on, and we gnawed on our Sulard's sugar cane until all the sweetness was gone and the stalks were chewed down to shreds. Me, Roscoe, LaVern, Benson, and Daryl, quiet, all understanding different things about the cold of that morning.

For Benson and Daryl, going to the market was a treat; they got to crawl all over the station wagon with no seat belts. For Roscoe, it was an opportunity to see if he could secretly look at the girls who went by. He didn't mind if they were black or white. On the Southside they were mostly Polish and German, and he knew if we saw him looking, we would make fun. For LaVern, it was just another unfortunate time that she was seen with her backward sisters and brothers. I gnawed nervously on my sugar cane, and wondered what Leland was saying to Deddy, wondered if I should have told somebody what I knew about Leland and Mama.

10

Letting Loose the Holy Spirit

The next Friday I got to get out of school early and went with Mama to my yearly eye appointment. The ritual was worse every year, with Mama's occasional touch to show a doctor or nurse that she took good care of me, and then the reading of magazine after magazine in a lamp-lit waiting room with mothers and children. I watched her hands flip pages until the little boy and his mother were called and we were alone.

Mama looked me in the eyes, and I felt her threat and looked away. "Why the hell are you watchin me read? Get a book and quit bein ignorant." Each year, this visit made her angry, and she strained to be good to me in public.

"Yes, ma'am," I said, and those were the only words between us for the four hours. I went home with new glasses. This time I picked out frames that were big octagons with tortoiseshell plastic. I thought the frames made me look sophisticated, but with my left lens a half-inch thick, my eyes looked different sizes.

When Devon and Gretal came down for the club meeting, Gretal took one look at me and said, "Odessa, you uglier than Mrs. Beasley from *Family Affair.*" I laughed with her to keep from feeling the pain of her joke.

Mama got dressed for the club meeting and carried Daryl into the girls' room, where we were preparing for our cousins by making a wrestling ring and finding the *TV Guide.* In her tight tavern dress Mama was round. Her large breasts bulged above her scooped collar. Her hips and butt pressed against the blue sequins. After seven kids, and weekends of club meetings, she didn't have the same smooth brown skin, but she was round in all the right places. With makeup to cover her bruised face, she looked beautiful like when I was little.

When Mama shut the door to the girls' room, Gretal yelled, "Anybody want to play Ella Mae?"

Gretal hadn't asked that in a long time. Lamont laughed out loud at Gretal, his voice deeper now. "Girl, you ain't never gonna get enough of playin that game. I thought after Ella Mae beat on you, you'd leave her alone."

We all started laughing, except for LaVern, who thought she was above playing the dozens. Gretal laughed too. "You just jealous because I'm two feet taller than you."

Laughter broke out again.

Lamont pretended to ignore her, letting his voice drop into a drawl. "'Ella Mae! Ella Mae!' Gretal, you the only country fool left who believes some crazy woman is hangin out in people's bathroom mirrors. I was holdin the door the day Ella Mae got hold of your butt. You couldn't get out because I wouldn't let you out."

Gretal leaped across the room. Her brand-new pleated skirt

flew up over her head, and in one wrestling move, she had Lamont on the floor, punching him in his arm. Her face was blotchy red with embarrassment and anger. Her cheeks filled with air to help her hold back tears.

Lamont was screaming and laughing in a high-pitched voice, "Ouch! Ouch! Oh, yeah, you're really hurting me."

Finally Gretal got up, conscious of her skirt and the way she straddled Lamont. She came and sat down next to me, and just stared at him like she was trying to make him explode.

He turned halfway around from the TV, still laughing. "You don't scare me, girl. Think you so tough. I got my eye on you too. You better not try to leave out of this room."

Lamont took pride in making Gretal break, in making her ashamed of being country when nobody else could make her ashamed of anything. He flexed his new muscles, knowing that, even though he was short, none of us was a match for him.

Lamont told me one day, "I know Gretal's weakness. She may be taller than me, but she hates it when she finds out that something she had all figured out is all wrong. If you wanna get her back for hangin out with LaVern, tell her something like, 'I didn't wanna say nothin, but Devon had you from sleepin with a white man.' It won't matter if it's a lie, 'cause she don't know who her daddy is anyway."

After the music was loud and the stomping had gone on for two TV shows, Gretal pinched me on the behind. "Hey, Four Eyes, I bet I can go out there and drink some liquor."

"And get your behind beat." I was learning to use Gretal's fast language back at her.

"Come on, go with me, unless you scared."

She chanted, "Four Eyes, Four Eyes," then stuck out her tongue and used her index fingers to make circles around her eyes. I thought about how with glasses I looked like a Goody Two-shoes, and how the one thing LaVern couldn't stand was when Gretal was being bad. So we waited until Lamont was in a trance, his eyes locked on the TV, and we snuck out.

We stood in the living room next to where Aint Fanny sat in the La-Z-Boy. Gretal was making fart noises in my ear. I was terrified of what Aint Fanny would do to her, but Aint Fanny was lost in the moment, howling out the blues the same way she used to shout in church. She was whooping and laughing at Mama, who was dancing with Deddy, both of them in the middle of the floor stomping and popping their fingers, their shoulders up near their ears.

Each year that passed, Aint Fanny got further and further away from her favorite saying, "The sanctified have God to get drunk on. Let every day be the Lord's day."

Eventually she just blended in to the Blackburn/Lacey picture more than Uncle Chet did. Uncle Chet still spent Saturdays fishing at the park, unless it was too cold; then he sat home in front of the console watching the football game. He ignored Aint Fanny's new behavior, saying, "The Lord will pull her back from her grief before she gets too far."

Ever since Aint Fanny started having evening wine before and after dinner, we got to see LaVern a lot more than Aint Fanny would have liked. "Don't be thinkin, just 'cause I let you baby-sit her when I ain't feelin well, that you can have my daughter, Bernice."

Her proper Detroit accent had faded and left her talking just like all the other aunts and uncles from Mississippi.

Aint Fanny sprang up from the chair to join Mama and Deddy. "Let's cut a rug tonight, y'all. Hot damn!" Gretal leaned her face into the seat of the chair, "Uuun, her butt stinks!"

"Shhhhh," I whispered, holding on to her pale, skinny arm,

trying not to laugh. I stared at the scene in our living room. Aint Fanny had her favorite church dress hiked up to her knees, her stockings drooped. She looked the same way when she was shouting in church, sweating, with her clothes falling away from her. In church, when she raised her dress and rubbed her thighs, the ushers swarmed over her in praise, because Aint Fanny was dignified and everybody didn't need to be looking up her dress while she was letting loose the Holy Spirit. But here in our living room, she was drunk and trying to do the Funky Chicken.

It all made me nervous and ashamed: the faded green La-Z-Boy with the brown tape still covering the place where Deddy cut it with his army knife, Aint Fanny's hands on her ashy knees, her stockings now down around her ankles, her legs opening and closing. I wanted to disappear, but instead my mouth flew open, my head jerked back. I exploded into laughter that pushed the waiting tears out of my eyes. I laughed loose, like Grandeddy and Mama.

Gretal grabbed a glass from the hi-fi, and we went giggling down the hall into the bathroom, where she drank the brown alcohol one sip at a time. She used my toothbrush to brush her cracked tongue while watching me out the corner of her eye.

"Why you always using my toothbrush without even askin?" I had calmed down to a grin now and was feeling close to Gretal.

"It don't matter whose toothbrush. I'm gonna rinse it out."

"Why you always brushin your tongue? That's probably why it's cracked." I wanted Gretal to know how it felt to have someone point out something different about her, like she always did to me, but she seemed unbothered.

"Nah, my tongue cracked because I had my mouth open when I was inside my Ma. Ma said I was probably tryin to talk from in there."

Even if I was trying to point out a weakness, like Lamont suggested, Gretal just took it as an opportunity to boast about herself.

"Uncle Loni told me that brushin my tongue is the only way to get all the germs out. 'Anybody can brush they teeth, but that don't mean they mouth clean.'"

I was so tired of how Gretal acted like she was closer to everybody in my family than I was. She spit in the sink and slurped rinse water out of her cupped hand, then turned to me with her hand on one hip. "You believe in God and stuff?"

"I guess."

"You cain't guess. Either you think there's a God who is lookin at us right now standin in this bathroom, listn'n to everything we say, or you don't!"

"I don't want to talk about not believin in God cause if I say no and there is a God, I'm goin to hell."

"But if there ain't no God and you spend all your time thinkin there is one, then you gonna be mad when you find out all this"—Gretal was getting red and exasperated; she held her hands out, gesturing to the walls—"that everything is a bunch of bull."

"Why you makin such a big deal out of it?" I rolled my neck now, annoyed with her. "Anyway, Gretal, you said you got baptized down in Mississippi. Whether there's a God or not, you got it made. But I'm gonna be in all kindsa trouble if I end up dead and in hell 'cause I never been baptized. At least you're saved."

Gretal laughed out loud like Devon when she was drunk.

"I don't feel saved. I feel like no matter how good a job Ma got, or what she buy me, no matter how clean my teeth is, no matter how many times I paint my nails, no matter how many times them old black women down at the beauty shop perm

my hair, I feel like cain't nothin keep me from sin and sin from
me. I just feel dirty."

We were only ten years old, talking like we heard our
mothers talk.

I tried to think about everything she had just said, but it
was all a jumble of facts about sin and nail polish and good
hair. "Gretal, I don't know what you're even talkin about."

She sat down on the edge of the tub and had to steady herself to keep from falling in. That's when I knew she was drunk
and talking out of her head.

I steadied myself too, stepping high over the crumpled bath
rug. I reached up and turned off the light and said to Gretal,
"Wanna play Ella Mae?" She giggled, limp in the dark, the
depth of her Mississippi twang full in her mouth. "Okay,
Odessa, but you gonna call her up this time, because I ain't
gonna have her lookin for me in this bathroom." She laughed
again and grabbed my arm to keep from falling over in the tub.

I stared into the mirror, frightened but giggling. I challenged her, "Ella Mae! Ella Mae!" There was nothing but the
thumping of club meeting music and laughter in the distance
beyond the bathroom door. I searched the mirror for her eyes
and felt the depth of my own, and there she was, her eyes hungry on me. I waited for fear to seize me, but warmth moved up
from my insides like the time I stood in the backyard, shielded
by the laundry hanging on the line, and lifted my shirt to let
the sun shine on my smooth brown belly. Her eyes were fierce
but gentle, familiar, and I let go of a cluster of knots that had
formed in my gut. I heard myself whimper and I reached out to
touch her face, but Gretal flicked on the light. My hand went
blunt against the mirror, and I stared at my own teary face,
searching for what I could no longer see.

"Come on, Odessa, I got to lie down."

"I saw her, Gretal, and I wasn't afraid. She was beautiful, like Granmama."

Gretal strained to look at me through the haze of her drunkenness. "Girl, what are you crying for?"

"I don't know, Gretal, but I saw her, I did for real."

"You gotta learn how to hold your liquor better, girl."

I dried my eyes and agreed with Gretal, though I knew that I had seen something, and it had not frightened me but had comforted me. We staggered from the bathroom and stepped back into the Blackburns' Friday night.

11

In the Silence

The next morning Mama held the ice pack to her jaw when she called Leland. When he got to our house, he picked me up. "Now, what a wonderful idea. If you want to keep them beautiful eyes for a long time, keep puttin them behind them protective glasses, keep anybody from stealin them." He chewed his gum, popping it between his perfectly white teeth.

"You don't think I'm ugly?" I asked, half smiling.

"You cain't be ugly." He laughed. "Hell, you good-lookin like me, and if you ugly, I'm ugly, and this country boy ain't hardly ugly." I giggled and took the stick of chewing gum he pulled from behind my ear.

Leland took one good look at Mama's face and announced in front of us kids, like he was doing a speech, "If you really want help, you gonna have to leave Loni, and let me work him out of where he's at with drinkin. Me and him got a whole mess of things we done had to live through, most of which I seen my way clear of. But my little brotha got all kinds of ghosts still chasing him, and cain't nobody really help him, except somebody he's known all his life."

Us kids scattered to our separate places. Lamont left the house with his football uniform and Towanda with her tuba. LaVern put her hair up in a twist and complained about how uncivilized it was for Baby Daryl to be picking his bottle up off the floor and putting it back in his mouth. Roscoe went to get his shoes on, anxious to get to the market, while Mama got Benson and Daryl dressed.

I went to the bathroom and turned off the lights. I whispered softly, "Granmama," but didn't see anything in the mirror except the outline of my own face. Outside the door I could hear Leland whispering to Mama, "Don't worry, baby girl, I got you," then silence between the sound of wet lips kissing. I stared at the bathroom door, trying not to breathe.

The door unlatched, and Leland flicked on the light. "What you doin in here, miss?"

He was happy, almost intoxicated. His mustache outlined his smile. He went over to the sink and started washing his hands.

I asked him, "Leland, sometime can you show me the trick with shot glasses and a peanut?" I was stalling so I wouldn't see Mama in the hall. He laughed big and said, "Girl, you kids don't never get sick of me doin them tricks. I tell you what, when y'all get back from the market, I'll ask your mama if you can come down to the tavern and see the place."

"Just me, not everybody?" I almost swallowed the piece of fingernail I was biting.

"Just you." Leland laughed at how shocked I was that he was going to let me see his tavern. Immediately, I thought about how this would top the Aint Fanny stuff and make LaVern real jealous.

Leland laughed again. "Now go on out of here."

I ran outside and got in the station wagon with everybody else. At the corner Mama turned around and sent me back in for the diaper bag. Inside I first heard bodies against the walls like thunder. Deddy and Leland were in the hallway struggling, Deddy's fist clutching a knife, desperate grunts, last breaths, sounds men don't allow themselves to make, and then he spoke. I remember that he spoke something very quietly before it happened.

If I closed my eyes and blocked out the sound of my own screams, of Mama running down the hall, of the click of the dead bolt on the front door when she doubled back to keep LaVern, Roscoe, and the boys from coming in, then I could almost awaken his words. Deddy's hairy arms broke time, my mind was begging, *Please,* but I did not move.

All I could conjure afterward was the color red, almost purple like the wine of communion. A dry burning beneath my skin, then eyes afraid, lifeless eyes, nothing else until the ambulance and the police car. We were standing on the porch, and they were pulling away, slow. I remember Mama's voice. "In self-defense," she said over and over, shaking her head, tears flowing like a winding river over high cheekbones.

That night, Mama scrubbed the floor with Comet, then bleached it, but the bloodstain pushed up through the puckered wood. In the morning she had men come and cover the floors with wall-to-wall carpeting. She said, "I'm tired of my house looking all shabby, and all kinds of company is gonna be up in here for the wake."

She moved the furniture, painted the walls, patched the dented places. High on a ladder that I quietly held, she reached above her head to the bathroom ceiling to patch the water stains. This numbed her and made her peaceful about the things we had both witnessed. But in my ears, sirens screeched all day, all night, to kill the demons in our house.

When we buried Uncle Leland, it was a beautiful fall day. The sun not quite warm, but white light where orange and red leaves showered the graveyard, headstones like bones jutting up out of the color green. Blackburns and Laceys, all of Mount Zion's children, stood like impatient birds waiting for Reverend Richards to break the silence.

My retarded cousin Neckbone rocked next to Grandeddy, mumbling, "Let's go in the car and ride, ride Grandeddy ride."

Grandeddy let Neckbone wear his overalls with a clean shirt and some dress shoes, and he wore the same suit he wore to Granmama's funeral.

Devon and Gretal stood beside Deddy like they were closer family to him than us.

Us kids stood with Mama and the aunts and their kids. Mama's face had been stern, a show of everything her and Deddy had said about Leland—"Think he better than everyone else." There was no sign of the passion that I had seen from the market stalls, the embrace, the sound of lips kissing on the other side of the bathroom wall. The woman I had seen through keyholes was invisible at his grave.

With her hands resting quietly on another unborn Blackburn, I wondered how she could so easily forget him— peace, she must have thought, untangled from her own messes, she must have thought. To be numb and pretend must have been her only comfort.

Three other huddles of people were there burying their dead. Their moaning, carried by the wind, swept over Uncle Leland's grave. Reverend Richards stood quiet, trying to still his mind before moving his congregation to a more mournful noise than the other groups in the cemetery. He searched his Bible for a passage to whip Mama and my aunts into a frenzy of tears.

"In these times when young men are being taken away from us like love stripped fresh from the breast of a new mother . . . it is hard not to think about death when we are scrubbing some-body's floor and not making enough to feed our babies, when we are at home trying to love our babies and they are showing us the evil in their hearts."

Mama and my aunts in unison, "Amen."

"It is hard not to feel like the life around us is full of death, but look around, look around! The Lord said, where two or three . . . I say two or three are gathered for me, there . . . I say there, I shall be."

"Amen! Say it!"

Reverend Richards's voice echoed off the granite. "Brotha Lacey is with my God. Gone home to glory land. Gloooory— hallelujah. He done laid his burden down."

"Amen, hallelujah, preach now . . ."

I heard moans coming up from the group of mourners behind me, who were there to bury some young man. They cried and yelled out loud at the sound of ropes lowering his casket—some black soldier's body resting in balance over his grave—and I remembered seeing on TV the bodies, stiff, in camouflaged hard hats, being dragged out of the death of a hot

Vietnamese jungle. I remembered my teacher Mrs. Farrell, her eyes swollen when we came in from recess and she was leaving for the day, on the verge of tears, not able to speak. The principal came and told us that her son was killed in Nam. And I remembered Granmama kissing my three-year-old mouth with both of her lips, then blowing on my cheeks—and then her face in that casket, her lips sewn shut. I started to cry for Uncle Leland, who would never smile that smile again, and for Granmama. I could still feel her chest against my ear, but in this gathering of family members, I felt untouchable.

Reverend Richards's voice came back, "For there is nothing hid which shall not be manifested, neither was any thing kept secret, but that it should come abroad." And all the aunts cried out loud.

I remembered the words of that verse I found in Granmama's Bible: "I had many things to write, but I will not with ink and pen write unto thee: but I trust I shall shortly see thee, and we shall speak face to face."

I turned to where I had circled it in Mama's Bible, and while the aunts were fanning to keep her calm, I tore it out, and took some comfort in knowing that when I was dead, I could tell Granmama about the things that welled up inside my head like pus in a wound.

That night I dreamed about Granmama shoveling in her backyard. She was looking for the flower bulbs that she had planted that didn't come up, and every time she turned over a piece of dirt, there was a hand or an arm. I walked off her back porch and tried to talk to her, but she couldn't hear me, she just kept shoveling like she couldn't see that she was disturbing graves.

I woke up sweating, and remembered a moment when I was five years old and sick with some kind of flu that made me ache between my legs. I pressed on my temples to stop the blood from surging through that part of my brain, to shut it all down before I vomited.

In the silence of my sleep I allowed my mind to step gently into the darkness of my memories. I was five, but I couldn't remember, and so I ran through songs, images of those days with still nothing but almost audible shadows, objects biting and pinching at my insides.

I managed to get myself to the closet to get my jacket and my shoes without waking LaVern or Towanda, and I crept quietly out the back door and climbed the stairs to Devon's flat.

It was before sunrise. The light of the moon washed over backyards and alleys. I tapped timidly at first, then frantically, on Gretal's bedroom window, still floating in the numbness of my dreams.

When she opened the window, she looked at me with eyelids still crusty. "Odessa, girl, what you doin?"

I didn't know what I had come for, until I opened my mouth to say to her, "Where is my Nakie doll, Gretal? You stole it."

"Girl, be quiet, you talkin out of your head like you crazy."

I climbed through the window, my skinny legs like tree branches in shadow to the moon. I went over to her toy box, rummaged through years' worth of doll arms, cars, and cookie crumbs, until I found my Nakie, still bloodstained. There I rocked Granmama's quilted doll and held it close, with shame and fear that I couldn't place.

Gretal sat watching me. She rocked nervously and asked, "You believe in God? If you believe in God, you don't have to worry, we'll see Leland one day." She kept rambling nervously about her understanding of death, until I was asleep on the floor.

She didn't tell anybody how weird I had acted that night, but she also didn't hang out with me at all that school year.

I was coming apart, like the stitching on my Nakie, who I now kept hidden in the back pocket of my jeans.

12

John 3:16

Winter came and froze the ground, and then spring softened it. The more things changed around me, the more I changed, until I could barely recognize myself. Regardless of the changes in me, the school year ended as it usually did. In June, Mama and Deddy reopened Leland's tavern and his neighborhood grocery and renamed them Blackburn's Bar & Grill and Blackburn's Market. Mama ran the store on one corner of Delmar and Goodfellow, and Deddy ran the tavern across the street.

That summer we went from being a family of nine who traveled in an old Country Squire station wagon to a family of ten—counting the new baby that Mama was going to have any day. We owned a new black Cadillac and a white van with a desert landscape painted on the side. Mama and Deddy just stepped in and made money off the places Leland had spent his whole grown-up life building, and Deddy was finally getting what he wanted.

Mama told me, "You gotta do right around here so God'll bless this house and yo new little brother."

Her words these days had a tone of revival in them. She pretended as though the sadness had faded in her, and left the hope of a better life with Deddy. Deddy could now afford to help Devon pay rent in a new apartment down the street and make our house into an upstairs-and-downstairs house. Mama was so glad to see Devon and Gretal go.

"Loni, now that you can afford to rent Devon her own apartment, why don't you just do that?" Devon was twenty-two years old now, and Deddy still took care of her like she was sixteen.

He was so proud of what he had that it looked like he got taller that summer.

"I ain't got to ask nobody for nothin now. Every mothafucka gonna be beholden to me."

He was grinning all the time, and when I came into a room behind him, I could smell the residue of musk left by his new confidence.

That day Gretal went back and forth up the porch steps to get her boxes of clothes and dolls and never looked at me, and I didn't confront her about it. I had scared her that night, and I had scared myself.

When Deddy had gotten all their stuff in the van, he sent Lamont and Roscoe down the street to help Devon unpack. He went down to the basement and got his sledgehammer, took it to the wall to make a doorway to the upstairs. Mama clapped and cheered him on: "That's right, Loni, tear it down! Tear it down!"

The upstairs was an exact duplicate of the downstairs.

Deddy turned the kitchen into a bedroom for Towanda. Lamont and Roscoe shared a bedroom, LaVern insisted on having the big bedroom right above Mama and Deddy's room, and Benson and Daryl got to sleep in what used to be Devon and Gretal's living room. The room where us girls had slept was now a dining room with new carpet, a big wooden table, and a wooden cabinet with glass doors. Mama made herself clear: "You see this, see how nice this dining room is? Don't go in it. When you want to eat, eat in the kitchen like you been doin." The improvements to the house were superficial. Some things got a fresh covering of carpet or wallpaper, but each piece of torn linoleum, each cracked and stained wall, was the imprint of an incident, and new clothes and furniture couldn't change that for me.

My sisters and brothers moved up to their new bedrooms. They seemed to have a new respect, or a new hope for Deddy, that I just couldn't muster up. I moved down to the basement. It was that, or share a room with LaVern, which hardly seemed worth it, since she was never going to stop acting like I was cramping her style.

She told Mama, "I can't sleep in the same room with her anymore because she makes me itch."

I was sick of her anyway, and tired of looking at her hair ribbons and bottles of perfume on the dresser.

Every morning that summer, Mama wouldn't let me go to the store to help; she only took Roscoe, saying he would keep her from having to stand on her pregnant feet so much. She said I was better off watching the boys than getting in the way.

"You too young to really help by ringin up things on the

cash register. Besides, I don't want you down there eatin up all the profit."

I stayed home with Benson, who was about to turn six, and Daryl, who was two years old now and was not only walking but repeated every awful thing he ever heard. If I slapped his hand for touching something, he wouldn't cry but hardened his face. "I'm gonna get a knife and kill you!"

One morning, I stopped Towanda before she could escape out the back door and off to band camp.

"Towanda, could you help me do the dishes?"

"I cain't. I have to catch up with Lamont. Have you ever tried to run with a tuba?"

"Maybe I could come with you and bring Benson and Daryl."

"Odessa, you know Mama don't want you leavin the house with them."

We paused for a second, and she recognized something familiar in my eyes. She recognized for a moment that I had changed, grown, since the last time she paused to talk to me. I saw her struggle with the conflict of her favorite saying, "Every man for himself."

She sat her tuba down at the door and said, "I'm always early, so I got a few minutes—ten minutes, to be exact, but this is the first and last time, Odessa. It's your turn to be the older kid watching the younger kids."

She hustled to scrape plates. She picked up the boys, stood them both up, and dusted them off like dishes.

"Things change, Odessa, and you have to get used to them like everybody else."

"It's just real different around here, Towanda."

"Yeah, this time last summer you and LaVern and Roscoe were tryin to figure out how to live with Mama sending y'all to summer Bible school down the alley at Ms. May John's house."

We both laughed.

"She was trying to save money on snack food, I think."

I laughed and looked over at Benson, who was still picking at the plate of bacon.

"Yeah," I remembered, "and we thought Benson was gonna be one of Jerry's kids, the way he was walking like he needed leg braces."

We both laughed at our family's backwardness.

"But it was all an act. That was so stupid. Then the clinic thought his bones were deformed because he was drinking too much milk."

I was enjoying her company, and glad that she had started a conversation.

"Odessa, remember that day that Mama was out back hanging clothes after taking Benson to the clinic? Well, I wasn't home, thank God, but y'all were down the alley, singing the Lord's Prayer so y'all could get your juice and windmill cookies and come home?"

"Yeah, then Mama noticed the refrigerator light on."

"She ran to the screen door, and it was locked."

We both laughed hysterically, recounting what Mama had told us, and what I had seen. The two of us in unison repeating Mama's words, "Benson sat down at the kitchen table and politely poured, and drank our milk for the week. He drank the whole gallon one cup at a time."

"I can hear Mama try'n to sweet-talk him, 'Come on, Mama's little scout. Come on, Benson baby.'"

"Girl, you lucky you weren't there. That was a long wait on the steps, with us locked out and him . . ." I was starting to get irritated now, thinking about the whole thing. How Mama spent so much time and attention on the boys before she and Deddy got the store and tavern.

But Towanda continued, lost in the humor of the story. "Remember, Roscoe thought Benson was possessed, because he started vomiting milk in clear liquid and white chunks. That's when Mama kicked the screen in and cried, 'Goddamn your little soul.'"

"Yeah, he sat on the porch repeating the verse he had to memorize for the summer, John 3:16—'For God so loved the world, he gave his only begotten son, so that whosoever believeth in him shall not perish, but have ever lasting life. Amen.'"

She finished drying the dishes, and I let the water down the drain.

The dishes were done, and I was back to feeling lonely. "Yeah, last summer was crazy, but at least everybody was here."

"Like who? Who ain't here who was here last summer? We just all have stuff to do, Odessa."

"Well, Uncle Leland for one. . . . I hate this summer."

"Well, grow up, Odessa. Our family is crazy. Fightin and killin each other, and the kids have to just find their own way sometimes. If you bored, find somethin to do like join the track team or somethin, then you won't be stuck, and Mama will have to figure out somethin else for the babies."

She had slipped out of our conversation, back into her matter-of-fact self. In two moves she shooed Benson out of the kitchen, slung Daryl into the playpen, and grabbed her tuba. "See you later, alligator," and she was gone.

There was only one day all summer when I wasn't trapped. Mama let me go to the store when Towanda was sick with stomach cramps and stayed home. Despite Mama's concern that I would eat up all the profit, I sat on a stool behind the counter and ate as much as I could in Leland's old store. I stuffed my face with what I felt Mama and Deddy had no right to. Whenever Mama went to the meat counter to slice baloney or braunschweiger and Roscoe was sweeping, I snatched a bag of Fritos off the clip and a Hostess cupcake off the shelf. I took a handful of corn chips and a big bite of cupcake, getting the salt and chocolate mashed up enough to swallow. The chips scratched the back of my throat, but I hurried and filled my mouth again. I did the whole snack in three mouthfuls, and I had five snacks that morning.

At lunchtime Mama had Deddy cross the street from the tavern to watch the store while she ran me home. I insisted that I was still hungry and took home a baloney sandwich. She was too busy that day with the store and the tavern to hit me or yell. She just kept her eyes on the road and said, "I cain't have you eatin all the profit."

13

Mulberry Tree

I had gotten tired of changing diapers and begging to go places with Mama or Aint Fanny or somebody, so I just started doing whatever the hell I wanted, and I didn't care if Mama got tired and told me to go get her a switch so she could whup my butt. The aunts told Mama that I was getting sassy and needed to have my butt whupped for breakfast, lunch, and dinner so I could even come close to acting like I had some sense.

One Saturday Mama called me in off the vacant lot where one of the nicest brick family flats in our neighborhood once stood. She yelled, asking me why I hadn't done something she had asked me to. She stopped pressing Towanda's hair, took the hot comb off the eye, and got after me with her bare hand.

"You think you too tough to cry."

"No, ma'am," I answered with a straight face, not budging while her greasy hand slapped my sweaty thighs. When she was done, I went back outside to the vacant lot, still without doing what she had asked. I felt justified in sharpening my stare, my tongue. Till now, I had no reason and no will with which to question my mother, but so many things had been lost.

To keep it certain that I was the child and she the adult, she took to slapping me and complaining about my behavior. This kept her innocent in my defiance.

I went to the lot and climbed up in the mulberry tree that over the years had grown as tall as the houses. I waited for somebody to come out and play. The branches were thick and low, the trunk was thick and sturdy, and the layers of branches went high enough for me to see backyards and the tops of garages.

I saw Mama come out on the back porch and yell for me, and I ignored her. I knew she couldn't see my brown face and legs mixed up in those dark green leaves, brown-gray limbs, and black-purple berries. I wasn't going to go in so she could make me feed Daryl or sweep up the hair, saying, "When you see somethin that needs done around here, just do it!" And then she'd get ready to leave for Saturday night at the tavern, and I'd be stuck with the little brothers I loved, but hated.

When no one came out to the lot to fetch me, I ate mulberries, and when I felt like puking mulberries, I threw some, trying to hit the same spot on the bricks of the alley. When I had made a big stain, I climbed down and wiped off the seeds and remembered Leland's blood on the wood floor in our hallway. I tried walking over the spot without feeling the stain. I smiled and pretended to be simply walking by, but each time I stepped on the stain, I heard Leland's head hit and crack on the hard floor.

Still no one came to the lot to make me go in.

So I stood silent on the stain until there was the sound of whiskey bottles breaking and Leland fell out of the bedroom door. Pieces of glass fell, muted. I stepped through the images until Leland got up to stop Deddy, then Deddy's knife connected under Leland's chin, the sound of the blade cleaving past flesh and bone. Leland fell back. His head hit the table in the hallway and made a cracking noise like Christmas nuts in Mama's palm. The knife spun in a pool of blood.

"In self-defense," Mama had said over and over on the phone, but now I remembered for myself. I stared down at the mulberry stain and remembered again Leland's wake: black, polished shoes stood in the hallway, the comfort of new carpet beneath their feet.

I stood in the alley. The afternoon sun heated up the smell of cans filled with garbage, and I hid my face in my shaking hands and quieted long sobs of shame for who I was and for having lost Leland by Mama and Deddy's careless hands.

14

Big Sister

At the end of the month Mama gave birth to the eighth
Blackburn. She thought at first she'd name him Edwin,
but when the aunts laughed, she decided to name him Jessie.
A week later Mama was back to the store in the day, and the
tavern at night, and I was left to change Baby Jessie's diaper,
rock him, and clean the navel cord that seemed to never fall
off. I hated taking care of the boys, but something about
Jessie's curly hair and round face made me think about angels,
brown baby messengers. When he was awake I rocked him,
while yelling at Benson and Daryl for fighting, and when he
napped I thought about escaping, and taking him with me.
When no one was looking, I did what Towanda said was
weird. I put my lips on his belly and made him flinch and grin.
He knew me better than he knew Mama. Benson and Daryl
had been weaned too early, but at least they had been breast-

fed. Baby Jessie hardly ever saw Mama, and this made me soften to him.

When the boys were napping, I went foraging through Mama's dresser drawers for change. The top drawer was the junk drawer—matches from other taverns, hairpins, garter snaps, pink hair rollers, pennies, empty coin wrappers, pages of old phone bills, sample tubes of perfume, crumbs, and loose food stamp dollars Mama now ignored.

I went down into the basement, turned on the washing machine, put whatever clothes were lying on the cold cement floor into the washer, and went out the basement door, up the steps, and was gone. My long rusty legs reached over the spiked top of the chain-link fence and scaled down the other side. I ran across the vacant lot, down the three steps that led to the alley, and down the alley as fast as I could run. My sneakers picked up speed, grinding broken glass into the bricks under my feet. I was on my way to Johnson Brothers' store.

Mr. and Mrs. Johnson owned the store down at the corner of our street and Byrd Avenue. Mrs. Johnson was a thin, dark black woman who reminded me of Granmama, except Mrs. Johnson was very quiet and spoke only when she was pushing her glasses up.

Mr. Johnson was a drunk. All the neighborhood kids tried to go in the store when Mr. Johnson was left alone. They would get more candy for their dollar, even though Mr. Johnson would slur, "You tryin to cheat me."

His speckled gray Afro extended down his face and under his chin, an Afro that was flat on the sides from where he had slept. His white short-sleeved shirts were always unbuttoned too far, revealing his collarbone and the hairs around his nipples. His frail veiny arms swung from side to side like a monkey's as he staggered to the cash register.

The smell of Pine-Sol diluted the smell of candy, lunch meat, and barrel pickles. The wooden floors creaked in every spot.

I went in to spend my dollar and was glad that Mr. Johnson was there alone. But I was disappointed too, because I knew it would take him forever to figure my change, and I couldn't stay long or else Daryl would wake up first and start pinching Baby Jessie.

Mr. Johnson sat down in the chair at the end of the glass candy case. His head drooped to one side; his mouth flopped open, as he supported his body with the arms of the chair. His long skinny legs were sprawled out onto the floor, his slacks too short for them.

"Mr. Johnson," I said softly, but he didn't answer. I stood next to the strip of chips that hung as far down as my arm. I thought about just taking what I wanted and then I thought about Mrs. Johnson, how her quiet eyes might be disappointed in me if they saw me turn from the quiet girl, the baby girl in the Blackburn family, to a thief. I thought for a moment longer, then snatched three bags from the clips, stood startled by how easy it seemed, and barreled out of the door, leaving the sound of the cow bell ringing behind me.

I went back to the mulberry tree and ate my chips. I sat on the highest limb and let my legs hang down. When I was done, I balled the bags up and wedged them into a niche between the trunk and a limb, licked my salty fingers, and scaled the fence quickly before the baby woke, crying.

15

Birthmark

The next winter Mama went to the hospital because she kept having tummy pains months after Baby Jessie was born. The doctor said she had to have gallstones removed.

While she was in the hospital, LaVern stayed at Aint Fanny's house, and Towanda had to stay late after school every day for band practice, so I had to do the shopping at the Big G Market, which was a few blocks past Aint Fanny's house in the nicer black neighborhood.

Deddy said, "You don't need a ride. A walk ain't gone hurt you none, might make you grow some muscles since you ain't growin nothin else."

I hated that Mama wasn't around to listen to Deddy talk because it meant Deddy was talking to me, and paying more attention to me than I wanted. He constantly said stuff about my body or how my hair looked, until I rolled my eyes; then he raised the back of his hand to me to make me flinch.

I tried to wear my clothes as baggy as I could. When Deddy looked at me, I could feel the space between my legs clench. He said, grinning at me, "I'm just kiddin with you, 'Dessa, I'll give you a ride to the store," but I ignored him because I knew that it was bait for him to later say, "I changed my mind, you can walk to the store."

Besides, I wouldn't have gotten into a car with him, but I listened to his offer and just said, "No, sir, I can walk." I walked ten blocks through the dirty snow every other day, and the sound of Deddy's ridiculing laughter spurred me on. I came home with pork chops, or chicken wings, or milk. Some days I let the snow seep into my boots to cool me off.

With Mama gone, Deddy didn't change his routine at all except he woke up every morning and expected me to have his breakfast on the table. I had to make breakfast for everybody, and all Lamont and Roscoe had to do was take turns putting out the trash, and Towanda was smart enough to leave every morning at six o'clock.

Despite all of her grown-up knowledge, Towanda misunderstood what was happening to me. "I'm glad you learned how to stand up for yourself, Odessa. I don't think you bein bad, I think you giving Mama and Deddy a run for their money, and they can't stand it. You the only one around here, besides me, who can see stuff for what it is." She slammed out the back door to catch the bus, and left me to make Deddy's coffee.

After breakfast was out of the way, Deddy made it a point to announce to me, "You ain't learnin shit up at that school that you cain't learn here changing diapers." Then he laughed, as high-pitched as he could, to get me to cry or complain, but I knew better, I knew that if I did, he'd just carry on longer. So I said, "Yes, sir," under my breath to everything he said, my face hot with anger.

After everybody was gone, I put on Towanda's church coat, which had a hood and draw strings at the bottom, and was twice as big as my coat. I wrapped Baby Jessie in his blanket, zipped him inside the coat, snug against my flat chest, put Daryl and Benson in their snowsuits, and walked Daryl to Head Start and Benson to first grade up at the school. I stopped in at the office to tell the principal that Mama was still in the hospital.

Mr. Stikes just said, "Okay, Odessa, you're a good student. I expect you to do your best to catch up when you come back." He was the only white person in our school. All the teachers were black, and I didn't want him to look at me and think bad of me. I wanted to tell somebody that I wanted to be at school, that my father had murdered his own brother, but I knew I couldn't tell him. I imagined what my aunts would say: "Don't be lettin white folks know all your business. They just lookin to believe we all got problems."

I wanted to go up to the third floor and see my teacher. I wanted Miss Clay to look in my eyes and know I needed something. She was good at that. One day she caught my eyes in the coat room, and came over to me, and with her slender fingers she held my chin and said, "Hold your head up, baby, and walk like you are somebody. Nobody can take away your pride in yourself."

I wasn't sure what she meant, but when I walked with Baby Jessie inside my coat, I practiced keeping my head up. I walked far and long enough to miss Deddy when he came home for his nap.

The day Mama had her gallstone operation, I didn't walk with Baby Jessie, because I wanted to be near the phone in case the doctor called, like on the soap operas when the doctor called to say, "I'm sorry, she didn't make it." I had been thinking a lot for the past few days, and was starting to feel like maybe Mama didn't say anything about what really happened with Leland because she was scared of Deddy, or scared that her sisters would think it was wrong of her not to stand up for Deddy, or maybe there was some reason that she needed to do what she did. I wanted desperately to believe that, to justify how she had behaved, and have her come home from the hospital and not die.

When Deddy came in for his nap, he walked past me in the sitting space. He stopped and stood over me. I said respectfully, "Hi, Deddy," but he didn't answer as he paced back and forth, each time blocking my view of the TV.

"Get your ass up and make me some lunch!"

This was the voice he had used so many Friday nights with Mama, the voice that was half muffled if I fell asleep with a pillow over my head, the voice that had boomed over me, mixed with Mama's hoarse breathless words after his giant hands turned my bed over, and spilled me and Nakie onto the floor like marbles out of a sack.

The hallway reeked of the whiskey and the musk of his unwashed body. My heart pounded in my chest, but I held onto my knees and stared at the TV. I drifted away from his voice and out toward images of myself in the mirror at age four, images of my face meeting the floor vent. The old cut over my left eyelid faded each year and got covered by Mama's voice, "Just a little birthmark." Her stories echoed off the walls in my mind. "Your birthmark was special, because it was where an angel kissed your bad eye and tried to bless it and make it better."

My head was filled with a million loud noises. Deddy's rough, dry hand collided with my cheek. Baby Jessie was crying now while Deddy yelled at me, his words broken by the collision of his fist against my face. "I'm gonna beat the shit out of you, heifer, if you don't get up and do what I say!"

I was down on the floor with my head covered. I was ashamed that I didn't pick up something and fight him back. His leather belt shrieked as he pulled it loose from his pants. It cut the air above my head and came down with all of Deddy's strength behind it. I imagined how this would all be remembered by Baby Jessie, who was crying so hard now that he couldn't catch his breath. He would confuse memory and retold stories. He would be afraid of Deddy's belts. He would open the closet only wide enough to get his church clothes and avoid the row of Deddy's belts hanging long, buckles shining. He would remember my bruised face and see me falling down enough imaginary steps to explain every mark on my body. My name would make him feel helpless, and I remembered—like remembering to breathe when I was born—I remembered Deddy's hand pushing my Nakie doll in between my five-year-old legs and ripping me.

Cold moved up my spine to the crown of my head. The only sound now was my heartbeat, and the sound of my blue jeans being violently tugged passed my thighs. I held my hands over my ears and screamed with my mouth shut—one long breath, until my head felt light and I flew through the ceiling, over rooftops, and landed safely in my classroom, where I sat patiently with my head down on my desk until it was over.

When I woke up, Baby Jessie was asleep with a bottle. I was naked from the waist down, my legs were still spread open, and a small puddle of Deddy's sperm was beneath me and sticky on my thighs. I grabbed my pants off the floor and clutched them to my chest.

The house was heavy with the smell of Deddy's stink; all the curtains and blinds were drawn and made the light in the house dingy like the air. I tried to breathe steady, but I felt like something heavy was pressing on my lungs. I put my hand over my own mouth and cried quietly so I wouldn't wake him in the next room. If I could get past the bedroom, I could get away, put my pants on as I got out the back door. But I couldn't leave Baby Jessie, so I slipped my pants on over bruised thighs and gathered Baby Jessie into his blanket to keep him warm. I held my breath as I inched passed Leland's death place, past the bedroom door, avoiding squeaky boards. But Deddy was not there; the bed was quiet, with covers twisted into odd shapes.

He had gone back down to the tavern, leaving me there to die, knowing that there was nowhere for me to run. If I told my teachers, Mama would tell them something different, about me being sick, or talking out of my head.

I wanted to be numb, to wash myself and not care about what had happened, to look at Deddy and be better at the game of forgetting than he was, look him in the eyes and make him wonder if those were drunken dreams about him doing that to me at five and now, about seeing me peer at him through the glare of my thick glasses with Leland's blood still on his hands.

The clutter of socks and shoes and the dreariness of the house made the pain of my head worse. I rocked Baby Jessie as I walked back to his crib. In my mind I heard one of the aunts singing a church song:

As I journey
through this land
singing as I go
Many arrows pierce my soul . . .

I managed to get myself into the bathroom by singing church songs. I looked at myself in the mirror and turned away. I looked like Mama with glasses, with cuts on my cheek, welts on my back. I touched the bruises on the inside of my thighs, and they had already turned hard and purple.

I had an hour before it was time to pick up Benson and Daryl. An hour to wash the smell of his sex off of me, to try to figure out what Deddy would tell my sisters and brothers about my cuts and bruises, and what I would tell my teachers. I ran a tub of water and eased myself down into it. I let the hot water enter and leave me to push out where Deddy may have made me pregnant. When I was done, I let the water down and started over.

I knew I had lost track of time when Gretal came banging on the back door with Benson and Daryl at her side. "Odessa, open the door!" I had already started dressing, but couldn't think fast enough to figure out how to hide my face. Baby Jessie was still asleep, his locks of hair sweaty on the side of his soft brown face. I hurried to the sitting space, where I pulled the rug over the damp stain of Deddy's sperm. I walked through the kitchen. The wood creaked under the linoleum, tired from the path worn over the years. After I opened the door for Gretal, I turned around as fast as I could. My two french braids were partially undone, and my body was clenched in pain. I could picture the scene of me scampering back to the sitting space, like Mama, hoping nobody would see my face.

Gretal peered at me in the dim light of drawn curtains.

"What? Did you just wake up or somethin? Hell, I ought to stay home and baby-sit too."

"Since when do you care, Gretal? I thought you found yourself some friends down the street." I had already made myself cold. I didn't want Gretal doing me any favors. After I had that nightmare, she treated me like I was just any other kid on Kennedy Avenue. Since then, she had grown two inches taller than me, and every time I looked at her now, I was jealous. Her hair was always permed, without a nap at the roots, and Devon let her wear it down in a Farrah Fawcett. Her blouses and skirts smelled like the department store, and her shoes were always shiny. Devon was working at Famous & Barr now, and all of Gretal's outfits were name brands.

Mama said, "That don't make no sense. When that girl get tired of wearin somethin, she just throw it in a corner and get a new one."

I turned on the TV for Benson and Daryl to watch *Sesame Street,* and Gretal sang the theme song while dancing with her hands in my face. I wanted to be strong and ignore her, but she stood in between me and the TV screen and got a good look at my face.

She stopped dancing. "Odessa, what happened to you?" The boys turned around. I grabbed her hand, and we went into the kitchen, where a stream of sunlight was bright on the kitchen table. She put her hand on the side of my face. "Girl, haven't you figured out how to stay out of your old man's way yet?" I focused out of my daze and stared at her. How did she know? For all she knew, maybe I fell down the steps again. She looked away from me, her almond eyes shaped by mascara and eyeliner. She was a woman at twelve, and she was Gretal, arrogant in who she was. She rolled her neck.

"Odessa, did he put his thing in you, or did he just beat you up? Did it ever dawn on you to stay out of his way?" I was crying now, in confusion over how she knew what happened but didn't seem shocked.

"Gretal . . ." My voice was hoarse, and I could barely talk through my gritted teeth. She put her hands on my shoulder and coaxed me like Mama, accusing and comforting, "I'm listn'n, you can tell me anything."

I started out defensive. "I don't get in his way! I do stay out of his way! I wanted to stay in the house in case they called about Mama! He did this when I was sick too, when we were taking a nap, remember, in kindergarten?" I knew I wasn't making sense to her anymore, but I wanted her to understand that I didn't do this on purpose.

"He put his hand and my Nakie in me, and Mama got mad." I remembered those days, how much I wanted Mama to love me, not treat me like something dirty. "Gretal, I forgot all about it by the time we went to all-day kindergarten. I didn't let him do it again! Do you think I want to be all beat up? Do you think I want to get pregnant?" I was trying to quiet my voice because I could hear Baby Jessie cooing at Daryl and Benson, and I didn't want them to get scared.

Why was I trying to tell Gretal, anyway? She thought she was better than me, just like LaVern. But as much as I tried to be tough, I knew that I was the weak one in the house, and Deddy was hurting me because he knew that if I was too scared to tell that I saw him murder Leland, then I would be too scared to tell anybody what he was doing to me. I let go of trying to be strong and slumped over in my chair and cried, and Gretal put her hands on my shoulders and cried too, and I was glad to have her there.

"Don't cry, Odessa. First of all, you cain't be pregnant till you start your period, and I know you haven't because your tits are too small. Besides, my ma said men cain't help it, especially if they stay drunk all the time. They forget who they wife is and takes to fuckin anybody. Puttin their dicks in people's mouths or butts. Ma say we just got to stay out that nigga's way."

I knew then that he had done it to Gretal too, and just like Mama, Devon had closed her eyes and moved out of the way, and pretended like it never happened to her or her daughter. But Devon still came to club meetings, she still grinned up in Deddy's face and took the money that he was always giving her in front of everybody—"Go tell Ranell and Racine what this motha-fucka got in his pocket." He made Mama and Devon think that without him they were never going to have anything, especially now that there was a black Cadillac and a van, something concrete to show the Blackburns and Laceys down South.

And now Gretal. She knew all of this all along, but it never stopped her from coming over.

"Gretal—" I wiped my nose on my sleeve. "Gretal, I saw Deddy kill Uncle Leland. I was standing right there in the hall and watched the whole thing. He found out that Mama and Leland had been kissing, and he killed him."

Gretal snapped out of her daze and reared back in excitement like she had just heard the latest from the soap operas.

"Aint Bernice and Leland was gettin it on?" She grinned now and threw her hand over her mouth.

"It's not funny, Gretal. Mama was complainin a lot, and Leland just sort of stepped in, and now he's dead."

She said back to me, smacking her lips, "Girl, you don't think it's hot, because you still a little girl, but when you a woman, you gonna understand a lot."

She wasn't a woman, with her makeup and understanding about periods and "staying out of that nigga's way." If she was any wiser than me, why was she here? How could she avoid Deddy for sure? We were twelve and had cried together about being done it to by my father, and we both knew that there was no one to really tell.

Memories of Gretal brushing her tongue, saying, "You can get all the germs off this way," memories of Deddy's hairy chest over me, penis, skin, blood, all swirled in my aching head.

16

Gallstones

Deddy declared that I was staying home with Baby Jessie until Mama got home from the hospital. At home I kept a cold towel on my face to make the swelling go down. The other kids assumed from Deddy's announcements that I had fallen down the basement steps again.

"I recollect you better either learn to keep your eyes on your feet, or you better not be thinkin you so different, and move on upstairs like everybody else. You more dented up than a run-over polecat." He laughed, and got all the kids to laugh with him. He stopped on his way out of the kitchen and cut his eyes over at me. I worked hard on doing what I had promised myself. I needed to look in Deddy's eyes. "Fire in them," is what my sanctified Uncle Chet used to say. But I wasn't so much scared of seeing that fire as I was scared that he would look in my eyes and know some part of me was dead forever.

The doctors had said Mama would be fine, and everybody was busy being happy that things were getting so much better in our family, but Deddy had stripped away any hope that things would be different for me. Until now, despite the pain of Uncle Leland's death, somewhere deep inside myself I had kept a hope—that with money Deddy would no longer be drunk and nasty—but that notion shriveled up like rotted seeds, ruined by the stink of Deddy's sperm.

The rest of the days of that week, I went to the store, and walked until I was sure Deddy had his nap and was gone back to the tavern. My right nostril was still split, and a streak of dried blood made a scab. The bruise on my right cheek pushed on the bottom rim of my glasses, but I concentrated hard on holding my head up. My teacher's voice—"Nobody can take away your pride in yourself."

On my way home from the Big G Market, I stopped at the corner store and was glad that Mrs. Johnson was upstairs. I would have given in to my shame if she had laid her quiet eyes on me, but Mr. Johnson's vision would be blurred and the smell of alcohol in his nostrils would drown out the smell of my blood dried in the cuts on my face. Stealing from him was easy that day. He dragged his feet around the store and talked about how much he liked the way I took care of my little brother, who I kept so close to my chest. The stolen chips didn't make Baby Jessie look any bigger inside my coat.

As long as I was in Johnson Brothers' store looking at comic books and reading my horoscope in the paper, my face relaxed into its childhood softness, but when it was time to go back to the house, I hardened behind the reality of cuts and bruises.

On my way out the door Mr. Johnson slurred, "Take care of that child. You smart—you sho smart."

At the end of the week Mama came home from the hospital. She was gray and smelled like medicine. She was swollen and colorless like Granmama in her casket. I felt like I didn't really recognize her anymore, she wasn't who I fantasized would come home and love me like I needed her to, and she wasn't the woman I was so angry at before.

She said to me, patting Deddy's side of the bed, "Come here, let me show you what they took out of my gallbladder."

She barely eked out her words, and I was afraid of coming too near her hands. I kept my fists in the pockets of my jeans and treated her like a distant relative who remembered when I was small. I went to her bedside with my face twisted in uncertainty.

She patted the bed again for me to come closer, but I didn't want her to get close enough to look in my eyes and see what I had done with Deddy. She glared at me sideways when she saw the scabs and bruises on my face, and then she touched my left eye, the eye that she took to St. Louis Children's Hospital to have dilated once a year, the eye that had become a free experiment for medical students who needed to see what impact could do to the retina. I kept my eyes on the pattern of flowers on the bedspread while she touched me for the first time in years. Her fingertips read blame through the scars that Deddy left.

"You got so big while I was gone," she said, remorseful, but the truth about who she really saw interrupted her need to pull me onto her bed.

"Go find somethin to do, Odessa. Don't just stand here staring at me like you ain't got no damn sense. Seein that I'm sick, you can go make yourself useful."

Mama held her arm cupped around her stitches and scooted carefully under the covers with her back to me. I rolled my eyes and huffed, angry that I ever let myself soften into wanting her to touch me. When she fell asleep, I came back into the room, crept over to the nightstand, where the gallstones sat in a clear plastic box, cold and outside of her body like me. I watched her breath steady, and wanted to climb in next to her.

17

The Baptism

That night I dreamed I was sitting on the back porch at Grandeddy's house, watching the wind blow through Granmama's sunflowers, a field of them tall and yellow. The clouds rolled in, almost purple with the heaviness of rain. At the bottoms of the stalks I heard something rustle and carried myself out into the field to see, but the sound seemed to always be just ahead of me.

When I was out of breath, I reached an opening in the field of sunflowers, and there beneath the light of the orange-and-purple sky was a freshly dug grave. I could smell the dampness of the soil heaped all around the square hole, and I knew that whoever had been rustling the leaves had been digging this grave for me. I started to run back to Granmama's porch, but couldn't find my way out of the maze of sunflower stalks. I woke up drenched in sweat and tears that stung the scab beneath my eye.

I wanted to call out for Mama, but I knew she couldn't save me. Loneliness pulled at my chest from the inside, and I cried quietly in the basement, beneath the rest of the sleeping house.

The next morning was a Sunday, and I asked Gretal to come to church with us.

"I ain't goin unless they servin dinner afterwards." Gretal laughed and did the Three Stooges slap at me, but when I didn't laugh, she frowned. "Damn, girl, you don't have to be so serious."

"I want you to go, Gretal, because I think I want to get saved, but I'm scared. I'm scared of standing in a pool of water with Reverend Richards, and me in some robe like a hospital gown. What if my glasses fall off, or my robe bubbles up in the water like what happened to Sister Hutchinson last month?"

We both laughed a little, and Gretal looked me in the eyes and said, "Yeah, I'll go."

On the first Sunday of every month, Reverend Richards didn't preach. Instead, more than half the service was dedicated to baptizing the children and grown-ups in the church who had not yet seen Jesus. The podium and the benches for the choir were moved from in front of the pool pit. From the pews the whole congregation had a good view of the sunken cement baptismal. It was the size of a kiddie swimming pool.

I entered the church and was always surprised to smell chlorine. That giant mural on the wall behind the baptismal— black Jesus being helped out of the river by two black guys— was uncovered and dominated the church with its power. My anxiety mounted, and I felt like the whole congregation stared at me when Reverend Richards called out the sinners.

"Some of you children of Mount Zion is old enough now to ask the Lord to save you! Do you love Jesus? If you want God today, come on up and get baptized!"

Then the whole church, including Gretal, started singing:

> *Take me to the water*
> *Take me to the water*
> *Take me to the water*
> *To be*
> *Baptized*

Mama and my aunts did ad-lib with their voices in perfect harmony, sharp and intoxicating. I started to shrink and hoped to disappear.

"Go up and take the preacher's hand and cry for your sins to be washed away," I heard some elder say.

On past Sundays, Lamont, Roscoe, and LaVern had gone up on a first Sunday, with their heads down in embarrassment, while the church swelled in "Amens" and "Hallelujahs."

Aunt Geraldine called out, "This is a spirited Sunday mornin," because already two of Mount Zion's children, younger than me, were standing at the pool pit, bug-eyed and nervous. The congregation got more and more spirited and changed the song by adding in a few verses.

Somebody who had already been saved got the Holy Ghost and started shouting and stomping out a holy fire, but all the sounds were muted now. I felt each second pass like days, and remembered Leland's casket on cold metal stands where the Lord's newest flock now stood waiting to be saved.

The whole church joined in, singing and clapping with the music. I couldn't avoid Reverend Richards' eyes anymore and started up the aisle toward the possibility of being washed clean.

He washed away
all my sins
and he made me
whole

Holy words and water, a spell that would make Deddy keep his hands off me—"In the name of the Father, the Son, and the Holy Ghost!"

I stood waist deep in the freezing water in a white robe that floated up to the surface. Reverend Richards' black robe was a giant balloon. He was in the water with his black slacks and his shoes. Aunt Geraldine stood at the steps that led down to the pool; her stout body blocked the way into the pool to keep me from running like a scared rabbit. Her glasses, giant binoculars, sized me up for my saving. She held on to the railing and reached with her white-gloved hand for my glasses. "Come on, now, you don't need your other eyes to see Jesus."

My hands were on each side of the pool, and I shook from cold and fear when Reverend Richards asked, "Do you love the Lord?" He held his white handkerchief up and waited for my mumbled reply before covering my nose and mouth.

Between dunks I clawed at Reverend Richards' hand to try and free myself. Despite the fact that over the years he had turned quite old and frail looking, he kept his grip and finished. Each time he held me under, his voice was muffled:

"In the name of the Father!

"In the name of the Son!

"In the name of the Holy Ghost!"

When we got home, LaVern and Roscoe were still laughing at me, and Mama was aggravated about how I embarrassed her. "You'd of thought somebody was tryin to murder your ass. Actin a damn fool." The scab from my face was now floating in the baptismal with the blood I clawed from Reverend Richards' hand.

I went down to the basement to be by myself and watch it get dark. I felt nauseous from the day, but safer than the day before. I was glad that nobody bothered to call me upstairs to help get the boys ready for bed. I curled up in my church clothes and rubbed the sickness in my belly.

The basement was the only sleeping space in the house that had a door that led to the outside. In the basement I could listen to Deddy's footsteps and tell where he was in the house. I learned the difference in everybody's footfall, the heaviness of a heel coming down, the stillness between steps.

There used to be a shelf in the cement wall where we kept our toys when we were little. But one day we came home from school and Deddy had taken a bucket of cement and filled in the shelf, toys and all—dried-apple-head dolls, comic strips, a Fisher-Price clock. I drifted off to sleep, remembering baking flat little cakes in the Easy-Bake Oven.

18

Skinning the Kill

The next morning I woke up with my bed filled with blood. For some reason, I had thought that my period would come like neat spottings. Gretal never told me that I'd bleed a river. In just a few seconds I had laid my tacky hands on everything in my room, trying to find something to stop the flow.

When I didn't come up for breakfast, Towanda came down and brought me some of every kind of period paraphernalia, and helped me clean up before going to school.

"You're an early bird, like me, Odessa. When you didn't come upstairs, I thought maybe today is the day." We ran back and forth to the basement sink, and she told me not to let Mama and Deddy know I was bleeding. "Whenever Mama knows I have cramps, the first thing she says is, 'You better not turn up pregnant.' No matter how many months I get my period, she says the same thing.

"And don't let Aunt Nell find out. You know how she is, like a old bloodhound."

Mama's youngest sister could smell the blood from a cut on someone's knee as soon as she walked through the door. If someone came in the room with a virus, or a runny nose, or blood oozing from any part of their body, she made her upper lip touch her nose. Then all the aunts would turn around to see who had been afflicted with what.

Deddy knew I had my period. For him it was another secret that he made innuendo and bad jokes about until I felt completely invaded. "Gal, you got something on the back of your pants," and then when I looked, he laughed out loud and got Lamont and Roscoe to laugh with him. He thought he knew me, but these days I knew that it was better to ignore him, or to laugh also to prevent him from weakening me. I studied his every move so that I would know more about him than he knew about me. I was never going to let him hurt me again.

He had taken to going hunting once a month with the other tavern owners in St. Louis. He bought every piece of hunting gear on the market. He said he needed all five rifles, "All for killin somethin different."

One Saturday I was still half asleep. It was about four o'clock in the morning. I could hear his boot steps echo in the vents over my head; then a truck with another tavern owner pulled up and blew, not giving a damn if the whole neighborhood woke up.

I waited, half resting, for Deddy to be gone. As I drifted back to sleep, I heard Granmama's voice say, *He'll come back with your blood.* I tried to force myself to remember this as the truck pulled off, and I slipped into the looseness of a deep sleep.

In the dream, Deddy called the house, and I was the only one home. He said for me to come to him right now.

He sounded both frightened and angry, and I hung up, confused, not knowing if I should go to him before it was too late, or leave him in the woods to die. I ran out of the house as fast as I could. Already I felt guilty for having paused so long. What if he was dead because of the few minutes that I hesitated? Did I want him to die?

I ran past Johnson Brothers' store, past my school, right out of the city.

Was that really what I wanted, for him to die?

I could see him in the distance sitting on Granmama's porch in Mississippi, rocking in her chair. When I got to the foot of the stairs, I had to bend over and hold my knees to catch my breath. I was angry that there didn't seem to be anything wrong with him, and that he had managed to get me alone again.

Our eyes met, and he said, "Get a bucket and wash all this blood off the walls."

I felt strong and solid in my anger, like running had strengthened the muscles around my heart. I stood there with the bucket and scrub brush and stared back at him, both of us shiny with sweat. Finally I dropped everything on the ground and said, "No, I'm not doin shit." I woke up and frantically searched for my Nakie doll that I now kept hidden under my mattress.

That evening Deddy came in drunk and laughed at his own jokes. He trudged mud all the way from the front door to the kitchen where I was cooking and doing dishes. Mama was there with me, shouting commands for Towanda to come downstairs and get Baby Jessie a new bottle, shouting for Roscoe to put out the trash, and shouting at me for everything I did backward while I was supposed to be cooking—punishment for not having the house clean when she got home from church.

I banged around the kitchen in response to her words, and rolled out and cut the dumplings. I could smell Deddy standing in the doorway to the kitchen, his hunting vest caked with mud. "Don't cook, I got dinner right here!"

In each fist he held a rabbit by the ears. Their paws were pulled in close to their bodies. Their fur, thick tufts to protect them from the cold. He slammed them down on the table. Flour went everywhere, and I controlled my reflexes, moved the flat dough over, and kept cutting.

Mama laughed nervously. "Now Loni, you know damn well I ain't cleaning that or eatin it. If I was gonna eat like that, I would have stayed down South."

"You ain't got to clean it. Dessa's gonna do it. If she big enough to cook chicken and pork chops, she big enough to see where real food come from. Come over here and get this knife out my pocket." He looked at me, but he focused on my forehead, not my eyes.

Mama said, "Go on, Odessa! I used to have to go catch the chickens out in the yard and wring their necks."

When Deddy was drunk and not angry, his voice was high-pitched. "If you won't do it, I will. But you gonna hold it." He laughed while he talked, and I knew Mama wasn't going to make him stop. Now that Deddy had more money to throw around, Mama didn't disagree with him, ever, and when things got to the point where he might hit her, she cupped her arm over her stitches to remind him that she hadn't fully healed.

I kept my eyes on him and dusted the flour off my hands. I

remembered what Towanda had said about Aint Fanny, how she picked on me because she knew I would cry or get my feelings hurt, that all I had to do was hide my weakness and act like she didn't bother me.

For the first time, I looked Deddy straight in the eyes and hid my fear with a look of slight amusement. I walked over to the other side of the table, picked up one of the carcasses by the back feet, and held it up for him. He stopped grinning and got serious with me.

He bragged about the last time he went hunting and shot a doe. "Hunt'n is all about the mind. If she gets scared of me, and let me know she scared of me, then she is as good as dead 'cause I'm gonna chase her all over them woods till she give up. But if I come 'cross a buck in the woods and he flares his nostrils, I might just think twice about whether he gonna lose his fuck'n mind and kill me."

He laughed, spitting beer out of his nose and into the new bushy mustache he'd grown.

Ever since he had done it to me, he took great pleasure in recounting stories about killing something female. He cut his eyes over at me when he was done, knowing that I was the only one in the room who took his story as a threat. As much as I studied him, I couldn't quite figure out if he remembered me standing in the hallway when he took his knife and cut Leland's throat. Our eyes danced around the vagueness of our memories and our secrets.

Mama spread newspaper on the floor under the rabbit as fast as she could, because Deddy had already pulled up a chair and started cutting around one ankle of the rabbit, then the other. He looked up at me. "Yeah, it ain't so easy to see where it come from. If you want to eat, you got to kill."

He pinched a tuft of fur on each ankle and yanked downward, but I squeezed the tiny bones and held my grip solid. When he looked up at me, I still held my face frozen, almost smiling.

By the time he had gotten the fur down to its neck, he was tired, and I think the smell of the raw flesh was making him sick. "Bernice, why don't you open the damn door? Cain't you see it's too fuckin hot in here?"

Mama kept her back to us and pretended to be doing the dishes. I made myself stay in my body—not end up somewhere else waiting for it to be finished.

The smell of blood conjured up memories of Leland's blood pouring out of his neck, the puddle growing bigger. It provoked the stench of Deddy's sex rising up out of the steam of a hot bath no matter how much soap I used. I swallowed over and over, forcing my mind to smell Granmama's perfume, the Afro Sheen in Baby Jessie's new silky hair. I pushed down the lump in my throat and talked to Deddy, so that he wouldn't find satisfaction in disgusting me.

"Deddy. Look. You can see all of the muscle."

He nodded and looked grim, pissed at me for not buckling. "Yeah," he agreed in contempt, then looked up at me with a new anger. "And I think it's a girl."

He stuck his knife into where she was separated between the legs and pulled down. Her guts spilled out onto the newspaper and onto his boots, rewetting the mud.

Mama walked out the kitchen door onto the icy back porch to keep from showing her nausea. Deddy stood up, looked past me, and still did not look me in the eyes.

"Now you such a expert. Clean this shit up! You hear me? Clean it the fuck up!" He pushed me out of the way and mumbled on his way to the bathroom, "Fucked up my goddamn boots."

I laid her and the other rabbit on the newspaper together, took them to the backyard, and started digging past the ice into the hard earth with a pitchfork and shovel, working fast to keep myself warm in the bitter November air of West St. Louis. Mama stood on the porch and dried her hands with the dishrag and clutched her incision. I felt like I should apologize to her for having acted so disrespectful, but I was pushed away from that impulse by her choice to be silent.

Dog yanked and yanked, and almost turned his doghouse over to get loose for the raw meat. I kept my back to Mama and didn't let my body shake while I cried and scooped Deddy's kill onto the shovel.

The Father, the Son, and the Holy Ghost, I thought over and over, knowing that my life was only as saved as the rabbits', whose stiff carcasses rolled off the shovel and into the hole.

19

Her Hands This Time

For the rest of that winter and the following spring I managed to stay out of Deddy's way. I discovered that the bus could take me anywhere in St. Louis or St. Louis County—from downtown where the Arch cast a shadow on the thick brown Mississippi River to Northeast Plaza Mall, which could only be reached by crossing St. Charles County—a flat, hot expanse of small farms and tornado-mangled trailers. I stole Towanda's bus pass and took Benson and Daryl and Baby Jessie in the stroller. I was too scared to steal anything from a department store but enjoyed the crisp smell of brand-new clothes in Sears and JCPenney. I window-shopped for hours to escape the dreariness I felt inside the house. At the end of the day I bought the boys ice cream with money stolen from Mama's drawer and told them we could go again next week if they kept quiet on the bus.

All summer Lamont and Towanda were excited, getting their stuff ready for going away to college. They had both won scholarships to Mississippi State University, Towanda in band and Lamont in football. Both of them floated in and out of the house like ghosts those days, trying not to do anything to ruin the peace that everybody else seemed to be finding, trying not to ruin their escape from the Blackburn family. After this trip to Mississippi, I might never see them again.

On the Saturday night before our trip, Deddy came home from the tavern drunk, and when Mama wouldn't let him into the bedroom, he kicked down the bedroom door. The next day I stood in the doorway of the kitchen, as tall as Mama now. She kept her back to me while she sipped her coffee. This was the first time since Deddy had Leland's money that Mama saw the old Loni rise back up to the surface. Probably her cheek or bottom lip was swollen. She mumbled, not knowing which of her children stood behind her, "I ought to leave that nigga."

I was glad that something had happened to somebody else in the family, that somebody else could see that Deddy hadn't really changed. I felt evil for not pitying her, and answered her with no respect. "Why don't you?" I asked, rolling my eyes, expecting her to turn around and smack me, but she didn't.

Mama looked out the screen door at Dog, who was pacing around his house. "Girl, I ain't got time for you. Tell Roscoe to get down here and feed Dog before it gets too hot out for him to eat!"

She walked over to the sink and dumped her coffee, being

careful to keep her back to me. "You ain't grateful for nothin, Odessa. Now Loni is providing food, and clothes, and a car nicer than most people ever had—"

I added, under my breath, "Deddy or Leland, I guess it didn't matter, long as you did good up in St. Louis."

She turned and came over to me. Her lip was swollen. We both stared long at each other, both maintaining a false calm, then her knuckles were magnified in my left eye. My lens crushed into the flesh of my cheek, my nose burned. It had all happened so fast. Another blow, harder than the first, slammed on my ear, and I felt myself weightless as the floor came up to meet me. The linoleum was comforting to my hot cheek. I could hear my own voice scream from far away, "Hit her back, hit her back!" but I couldn't.

When I got to my feet, I counted inside my head—counted the number of running steps to the basement door, and then the number of steps down the basement stairs and to my bedroom. I opened the door and used my free hand to drag my bed across the cement floor.

I crouched down and pressed my back against the foot of the metal bed and pushed the bed to the door, my feet flat on the wall, my knees locked, my nose and left eye crying red. I screamed for her, "Mama!" over and over. Her stub legs kicked the door. The tenor in her voice went hoarse, the metal of the bed rattled against my shuddering body. I screamed her name, but the cinder block walls absorbed my voice.

I never heard anyone sing like Mama could sing. Three-part harmony coming out of one mouth. She was sharp and clear, and her tone almost cut you in half. It was nothing like her yelling.

Her singing woke me. Someone had moved my bed back and put me in it. I couldn't open my left eye, and my right only gave me the dim light that made its way through the window and into the basement. The fuzz of Mama's brown silhouette walked back and forth over me. I wanted to reach for her comfort. I hated myself for wanting her, and hated the way I must have looked, swollen by her hands this time.

With Deddy I had learned to stay out of the way, but I had craved Mama's touch since the time I knew words, before walking and crawling. I wanted my mother, and I wanted my grandmother, whose touch was now ten years in my memory. For now I took comfort in the familiar pain of Mama's singing, in the familiar lies that she was conjuring to right the recent past.

"Glory-glory Ha la loo ya—since I laid my burdens down—"

I could tell she was smiling—smiling like she smiled in the choir stand at church, like the words were stroking her heart, filling her with light. I heard Benson and Daryl run across the floor, over my head. I raised my heavy hand up to touch and see if my head was all together, or if it was lying broken on my pillow.

"LaVern, bring me some more ice. Sleepyhead is finally waking up." Mama clapped her bare feet against the cool cement floor, a rhythm that sent me back into a cold sleep, where Mama's voice came steady.

"She done fell down them stairs again," and on command I saw my own body flailing through the darkness and landing in a pool of storm water.

In my sleep that night I heard Granmama's voice say with urgency into the darkness of my mind, *Keep your mouth shut, child. Keep your mouth shut!*

20

The Last Supper

On the way to Mississippi I hid my swollen face from everybody. I was lonely even with seven sisters and brothers. I wished Gretal hadn't gone to summer school but could be there with me. The two of us would have gone off behind the house and talked about Deddy. Ever since he had done it to me, Gretal rolled her eyes behind his back and whispered to me, "That dirty bastard." The two of us made things better by mocking the way he walked, the way he talked. I missed her.

My sisters and brothers fit well in the new van. They swiveled around in its bucket seats and took turns sitting in the back because it was like a couch. The portable TV aired sitcoms through static, and they laughed and were so content that I felt ill and stared out the window, refusing to talk to anybody.

Mama let Baby Jessie sit with her in the front seat, and only passed him back to me when he needed a diaper change. When

I complained that I wanted him to sit with me, Mama said out loud into the van, "Seem like things got better, and Odessa started act'n worse. Some people comfortable with things how they are even if things are bad."

I rolled my eyes. She knew why I had become so disrespectful, but the more I rolled my eyes, the more they all said, "Odessa, don't be try'n to ruin everybody else's trip."

I watched the back of Deddy's head and thought about Achilles in *The Adventures of Sinbad*—the indentation at the nape of Deddy's neck, maybe the crown of his head. Where was his weak spot? Someplace where bone did not cover him. I remembered Uncle Leland's words, "When a man's got to have his drink, ain't no amount of money or noth'n else gonna stand in his way." For the rest of the trip, I calmed myself with the fantasy of taking the beer out of the cooler and hiding it under the seat, leaving Deddy with two hundred long miles to Grandeddy's whiskey.

The next day, I quieted my thoughts by counting. I counted the ridges on the butt of Grandeddy's rifle, the keys on Granmama's old piano, how many white keys and how many black, the number of broken keys, then missing keys. My tongue counted teeth. My eyes, the number of trees they could see near and far in the flat dust for a mile around the house. First nine, then eleven, counting the tree bench.

The rain in the distance beyond the eleventh tree came down and beat the dirt. A cloud of orange dust moved toward the house. I imagined a herd of cows gone mad. The smell of rain and dirt rolled over me on the porch, then over the house. For a moment I was in the cloud and pushed with the herd to roll the air forward. I ran toward myself, on the porch in cutoff overalls, dirty blue like the sky. I felt sorry for who I was, and ended my fantasy just before I ran headlong into myself. On the porch I counted the number of drops that had already fallen on the weathered boards of the steps.

I remembered looking at someone in this spot, and me on the bench. It was Granmama, and I was three. I walked off the porch, out into the rain. I wanted to put my busted eye on the other side of the eleventh tree.

When I got past the trees and beyond the ditch where Grandeddy dumped the apple peels and cores, I turned around and saw Grandeddy's house, the road to the store, off to the right. My cousin Neckbone tiptoed over wet rocks on his way to the store where he napped all day behind the Coke chest to avoid the heat. Uncle Jo's house was smaller than it ever looked from Grandeddy's porch.

Everything looked small. I counted three buildings from left to right, then right to left. I wanted to count them in every way before thinking again. But my mind was slipping past the sound of my feet running from the store to the house, the feel of dew damp on the rocks and cold on my feet, the sound of the rope steadying Granmama's casket into the ground. I could smell the dry dusty yellow of Granmama's sunflowers behind Grandeddy's house in the spot where now lay dry cracked earth and the remains of some bird that Deddy had shot out of the sky early that morning.

My mind got noisy with rain and the sound of forgotten days in Mississippi. Then I looked at the house and realized that except by car, I had never ventured off Grandeddy's land.

I imagined myself a runaway slave who wasn't sure if she should approach the houses or stay brown and safe behind the tree trunks. I lingered there until the sun vanished behind the store, and Mama called everybody for dinner.

That night we all sat on the edge of the porch. The light from rusted buckets of citronella candles drew some of the mosquitoes away from our feast. We held our plates in our laps, and all the kids and grown-ups talked and laughed, while I swung my feet to the rhythm of chirping crickets. I felt the occasional warm breeze surround and separate me from the others.

The next morning was thick with humidity and heat. The air was sweet with cow manure, wet hay, and Grandeddy's whiskey. Everything was quiet, even Grandeddy. On most mornings he sat up on his bench in the store, hooked his fat thumb behind the one buckled strap of his overalls, and started Diana Ross low on the jukebox. But even he was quiet behind the distant black eyes of the store.

Mama was the only one awake. I crept into the kitchen, trying to keep the creaky boards from startling her. She half talked, half whispered, "I used to walk in my sleep."

She stood at the stove, already dressed in a terry-cloth shirt and jeans. Her hands braced each side of the stove, and I wondered if she was talking to me, or to the four steaming pots of water.

She went on talking. "One morning I got right up out of bed and took Nell by the hand and made her come too. I woke up when Motha came out on the porch. 'Heifer, where you think you goin!'"

I hated when she did Granmama's voice. I was sure it wasn't shrill, and I can't imagine her ever cussing. Mama laughed, her rolls of fat moving under her shirt. I sat down at the old metal-rimmed table that looked so much like ours, but more worn, and Mama joined me. I didn't want to be this close to her when everyone else was asleep, but I fantasized her telling me she was sorry for hitting me. I fantasized that she would see my swollen face and know that this time she had done it, and maybe she would comfort me and hear my words, "Deddy did it to me," and then she would leave him—no more hopes that he would be good to us.

Mama snapped the beans for that night's dinner. "Where'd you go yesterday?" She reached and the enamel bowl spun, clanking three times before I answered.

"There wasn't anything to do when Neckbone took his nap, so I went outside."

"Outside where?"

"Near the tree bench."

"Quit lying. It was rainin."

"I went to Grandeddy's ditch to get the peels and stuff out. The goats had been finish eatin. I didn't want the rain to get stopped up in the ditch."

"Where'd you put them? Did you see Loni while you was out there?" Her tone was accusing, and I watched tension stiffen her hands.

A hard lump formed in my throat and made it hard to swallow back tears. Mama snuck up on my weaknesses before I could think to hide them. She broke me with her scorn before I could think to defend myself. So I let my mind drift away from her accusing tone.

How did Mama get in off the porch other nights when she sleepwalked? How many kernels of corn were there in the ceramic cornstalk that hung near the back door—seven, eight, nine? How old was she when she painted it? Where was her school? Did Granmama press her hair on Saturday for church on Sunday?

"Don't you hear me talkin to you?"

The muffled humidity quieted her.

If cows had really flown over my head in the gray of yesterday, and if they had been visible, how many of them, what colors, with wings, or did they just float?

The lump in my throat dissolved. My face felt cool, and I remembered a cold white rag when I was three years old, and I was the last Blackburn kid to get chicken pox. Mama's open hand was rough but comforting.

I was humming with Grandeddy's jukebox now, "Baby love, my baby love . . ." Between the croons of the Supremes, Mama's words faded.

"You better not turn up pregnant! You hear me? You better not turn up pregnant!"

I didn't see her get up from the table or slap me. My cheek stung against the flesh of her hand. The black enamel bowl was spinning, empty, and it was over.

Mama bent over the stove to pour the last of the string beans into the four steaming pots. "Get up and go wake them kids up."

After waking Benson, Daryl, and Baby Jessie, I ducked into Grandeddy's bedroom, grabbed Granmama's Bible out the nightstand, and stuffed it in the back pocket of my overalls.

On my way to the door I lifted Roscoe's ashy legs and slid his Keds from under him. The rug on the living room floor was musty and worn over the dampness of the wood. Little by little everything in Granmama's house had become worn, and shrunken under our growing bodies. Roscoe lay tangled in covers on Granmama's old rug of the Last Supper. His head and feet now extended past the frayed edges. Dragging his Keds wore another spot next to Jesus' open hand.

There was nothing in Granmama's house for me. Snap peas, and Mama's anger. I leapt over the Last Supper and banged through the wooden screen door, reminding myself that my own Keds had a hole in the right toe, and Roscoe wouldn't need the reinforcement as much as I would in my escape. Shoes in hand, one overall strap still unbuckled, I ran over the rocks toward mud and eleven trees that could vanish me for the day.

21

Beyond the Eleventh Tree

From my hiding place, I watched Mama do the job she had left me to do at home—bathe the boys, feed them, stare at them from the front porch. She kept one eye on the boys and one eye on Grandeddy, who might be looking at how wonderful a mother she was. I watched her eyes follow Deddy. He came out on the porch in clean slacks, white short sleeves, and a straw dress hat. Grandeddy whistled through his teeth, and Deddy whistled back. Mama laughed and stood beside him and called everybody in for lunch, even me. Deddy moved past her, down the steps, and to the van with kids moving past him, but not touching him.

The sun began to burn through and filter light down through the trees. Lamont came out on the porch with a soda that I was sure was root beer, the only kind he would drink, the kind that made my throat so slimy I couldn't swallow. He turned the bottle up and didn't let it down until he was done.

He wiped the sweat off his forehead, and I was sure he was staring at me when he walked to the edge of the porch, where he cleared his throat and spit several times. I could see what there was of muscle in his arms. He was almost nineteen, and though short for his age, his body was thick with maturity. His jeans were slightly worn where his penis rested.

The sun rose up above the trees and burned away the last moisture of morning. The smell of red and brown mud made my mouth water and reminded me how hungry I was. With my back to the eleventh tree, I looked straight up through the thick brown branches and imagined Leland's arms lowering for me.

The cracks in the trunk were like curvy highways; ants passed politely, not touching. I rested my lips on their world and thought about them moving in the valleys with my breath making warm wind. My chest felt numb against the bark, my right breast covered with T-shirt and overall, my left breast T-shirt against bark, both numb on my body like my lips after Mama's slap.

The kids came back out, and Baby Jessie yelled my name, "Dessa!"

I peered from behind the tree to see him in the yard, only dust and the bars of his playpen separating his eyes from my hiding place. He could see past the noise of kick ball, the goat calling her kid, the jukebox. I wanted to answer him and put his curly hair under my chin, his sweaty forehead on mine, but the field of rolled hay behind me pulled—a new quiet place, maybe somewhere to lie down and nap in the day and not be seen. If I stepped out for him, there would be no more walking past the eleventh tree. Mama would beat me, and for a second I stared at him and was jealous of his smell, the smell of new life, hair still shiny from the food in Mama's blood.

Hungry for lunch and more quiet, I ran away from Baby Jessie's voice and onto someone else's property. There I scrunched behind the hay and held my knees to my chest. The sun made my brown skin hot like tar. I hid my lopsided face on my knees, tears for Mama not to find me, and for Baby Jessie not to cry for me. Snot and tears made mud out of the caked dirt on my knees. As the sun slowly arced and dimmed to crimson, I forgot about Mama and Baby Jessie and transformed the field of hay and myself into many wonderful things in my dreams.

22

Through Rows of Rolled Hay

A deep voice called me out of hungry dreams. It was far away at first, but then closer. "Whose child are you?"

I smelled the air of night coming, and hay poked through the back of my overalls, but dreams of moon pies and cornflakes pulled me away from the voice and back toward a deep sleep. A hand reached inside the thick liquid of my dreams and snatched me up. My eyes strained to register the reality of shadow, the absence of daylight. With every beat, my heart pushed into my throat like the jawbreakers I was always swallowing.

Before me stood a grown-up silhouette that was thick and smelled like Mama when she sweated. The sky left only enough light to remind me of blue. "You Bo's kin?"

"No," I answered without needing to think. Grandeddy always said if anybody is to mess with us around his place, just say no when they ask if we know him.

"What you doin sleepin out here?"

I shrugged my shoulders and left them huddled around my ears; my hands made fists in my pockets. I knew I was in trouble for being on somebody else's land, for not going back to the house before dark.

"Well, if you don't say somethin soon, I'm gonna just keep on my way and leave you out here for the mosquitoes."

The shadow turned toward the fading light, revealing breasts, and I lowered my tense shoulders.

"I'm Odessa."

"Whose child are you, and what you doin out in these people's hay?"

"I caught the bus here from Chicago to visit my aunt," I lied, and saw in my mind people and settings that didn't really exist.

"What's your auntie's name?"

"Oh . . . she's dead. The Laceys told me that the old shack I was tryin to get to had burned down a long time ago." I blinked and rubbed my sore left eye under my glasses. I wondered why I wasn't being more careful with my lie. Using Mama's maiden name was almost as good as telling the truth.

"But what was your auntie's name?"

"Uhh, Elizabeth." Before thinking I blurted out Granmama's name and realized that this was the first time her real name had traveled through my body and out into the air with my voice behind it. I hoped the shadow of this woman didn't know my family well enough to consider how little sense my story made.

"Yeah, that be just like them to be talkin about somebody dead." Her silhouette spit snuff out into the field, and the last of blue sky gave in to black.

Her voice was warm and sweet like the dampness of the

hay. In my mind her thick body shrank to fit the calm of her voice. The only lights now were the three points behind me— Uncle Jo's house, Grandeddy's house, and the store.

"Well, you cain't just stay out here in the dark talkin about lookin for folks you say is dead. Come on home with me and get some food in your belly."

In the darkness I listened for her steps. Her smell was not like Mama now, but distinct, like Granmama's. I reached out for her hand, which was thick and rough, and pretended I was three, reaching for the hand that was thin and textured by sun, the hand that closed around my round fist years ago.

Twice she pried open barbed wire for me to step through, and twice I cut my shin.

After a while I was used to the dark and to the size of her figure forcing into the invisible space. We seemed to be floating in a rhythm, changing lead and follow as she separated weeds and wire for me to step through. I fantasized the gates of hell at the end of this journey; the devil laughing and thanking his giant wife for bringing me home.

I thought of how this would end in slaughter, like the child molestation movie at school. It frightened me that even though I had these thoughts, my heart was calm and my breath seemed cold on the sweat of my lip. I didn't care where I was going, just that I was. For a moment I wondered if my body really lay dead behind the roll of hay.

She said to me, when we reached the three steps of her porch, "You here now. Anybody ask who you is, tell them you Elizabeth's kin. They ask you what you doin here, you say hanging out."

A brief image of the fading photograph of Granmama flashed behind my eyes while she spoke. I thought maybe she had looked into my eyes and called out my Granmama—a trick to get me to be friendly with her.

"Why am I supposed to say that?" With my head cocked to one side I waited for her response. She only looked back at me with the gaze of an angry dog, and I could not stay strong and stare her down. In her eyes I could see that she knew I was weak and afraid, and that I had not wandered around looking for the house of some dead aunt, but had very quietly walked away from being a Blackburn, putting darkness and barbed wire between me and them.

"You supposed to say that because you say you was lookin for me, so here I am."

I was confused and wasn't sure if she heard and understood me. But I didn't want her to know I was uncomfortable, so I held my neck-rolling stance. All I could see of her now was her height and the whites of her eyes. I said my name over and over to myself to avoid her spell. I made myself sound tough, like Gretal. "You don't know why I came here."

At this she turned and ascended the stairs. Her figure melted into the vastness of dark all around me.

"It's dark," I whined into the space that grew between us. Her footsteps rested, and her voice came steady like her stare.

"It's never dark."

The wood frame of the door clapped behind her, striking up the song of crickets and cicadas. In that moment I realized that I feared seeing her face. I feared going inside, staying outside, attempting the walk back to Grandeddy's. I was nobody who was nowhere, and I didn't feel strong any longer.

I pushed all thoughts of Baby Jessie's crying away from me and felt my way up the stairs. On her porch I groped in the dark and found a cushioned bench that smelled strongly of mildew. There I lay down on my side and stared. I listened to the silence behind the invisible walls of her home. I thought that maybe nothing lay behind the walls, endless nothing, and no one had ever led me away from the haystacks. I lay clenched and pushed back the need to cry. My eyes stared out at nothing until eventually the darkness offered up a crape myrtle with blossoms that glowed. It stood silent in front of the porch. It was then that I closed my eyes.

23

Fifth-Born of Eight

When I woke up, she sat on the stairs with her back to me, long dark hair and broad shoulders. The air was much too heavy and damp for the denim jacket she wore. I lay still and observed her masculine movements, the way she picked her teeth with a piece of straw, and I wondered how I would leave the porch without her seeing me. Her voice rang out deep and solid, "Good mornin!" I didn't answer, and she didn't turn to me. The sound of one lone whippoorwill's call swelled as the silence between us grew noisier. "Good mornin!" and she turned to me. Her face was as much like any man's as I had ever seen, angled bones, reddish brown skin worn by the sun, like the dirt that settled on the stairs of her porch. Though she looked like kin whose faces were stored someplace distant in my mind, she looked like no one I had ever seen before.

"You ain't got to be scared of me, child. If I was gonna bite you, I would've done it last night while you was snorin loud enough to wake up the cows."

Reluctantly I smiled, but quickly blanked out my expression.

She turned around. "My name is Elizabeth, and despite your lying, I know I done stumbled upon one of Bernice and Loni's chil'rens." She went on talking, but my mind was stuck on "Elizabeth."

My head pounded, and I got to my feet and said in a very direct manner, "I think you should walk me back. I'm already gonna get the beatin of my life for being gone. It's even too late for makin up a story."

"Is that how you got that big black eye? Look like from what I can remember folks ain't supposed to punch somebody who wear glasses." I was on the edge of crying and got up to push past her massive body and the crape myrtle. But her smell went with me. It was the smell of her sweat, of dirt, of the hem on Granmama's cotton dress.

I thought I could hear Baby Jessie in the distance. I could feel his eyes still locked on me beyond the trees. On the way to Mississippi I had wanted so desperately to disappear, to leave them all in their happy van and to simply disappear. But now I wanted nothing more than to take a hot bath and listen to Towanda go on and on about Mississippi State, hiding her fear of leaving. I wanted to look at LaVern's turned-up nose and know that who she was helped me to understand who I wasn't. I missed Baby Jessie's new smell, still like milk.

What if they leave without me? What if I die here? I started to run, but I stopped before reaching the broken-down wooden fence at the edge of her yard and realized that when Mama got me alone, she would do more than yell at me. I would be slapped or whupped with a green switch from behind the house. And Deddy would come out and beat me like I was his wife, not wanting to lose me under his strength, but strike me just hard enough to leave his mark and to show Mama that he could succeed at hunting me.

I turned to Elizabeth, who was standing on the porch now, and for a moment she was Granmama, but thicker and more stern. None of the sounds in my head, the impulses to run, to speak, nothing was kin to anything else. All the things I wanted to use to steady myself—the counting game, the songs from church, Motown records—all ran into each other in my head. Elizabeth paced the porch and ran her fingers through her hair. The rhythm of her boots and the squeaking boards comforted me and frightened me. Someone with no place in my world hovered. Her presence had shifted my family tree, leaving the lives and deaths of hundreds of relatives scattered about in my mind.

Elizabeth struggled with her words and shouted from the porch to break my trance. "Well, whether you is goin or whether you ain't, you ain't had nothin to eat, so come on in here and let me fix you somethin."

I was dizzy with hunger and let myself fall to my knees. I felt like I was going crazy. What was this place, and who was this woman with Granmama's name?

Elizabeth's hand was rough but cool on the back of my neck, where already the morning sun was baking me. She sat down in the dirt next to me and started talking, her voice dark and quiet.

"They ain't good to you at all, is they?" I didn't answer but kept my face down so that she couldn't see my nose running.

"Family supposed to be good to you, but they be the main ones to keep you chained up and scared to death.

"And when your own kin hurts you, it hurt worse than the same transgression comin from other folk."

I wasn't crying anymore but said into the curl of my body, "Why do you have my Granmama's name? Are you her?" She laughed, deep and hard with her head thrown back like Grandeddy.

"I'm her daughter. Don't you remember losin your Granmama?"

"Yeah," I said back defensively. I hid a smile. I knew she was my kin.

"Sit up here, now. You ain't gotta be cryin about nothin."

I sat up, and the two of us stayed in the dirt with our backs to her rickety wooden fence until the haze of morning gave way to the stark Mississippi sun.

Elizabeth reached in the breast pocket of her jean jacket and pulled out an old black-and-white bandanna. "Clean your face."

I took the bandanna and reached in my pocket and pulled out Granmama's Bible, all rounded off by the photos that bulged from the inside.

"I know Granmama's dead, but I didn't know you. Nobody ever said anything about an Aunt Elizabeth." She reached over and engulfed the Bible with her massive hand.

"They don't call me Elizabeth. They call me Ella Mae."

She turned to the first page of the Bible and said, "See 'Fifth Born of Eight—Elizabeth Mae Lacey,' and right here next to it, 'Ella Mae.'"

I shielded the sun from my eyes and glared up at her.

"Nobody ever said anything about any Aunt Ella Mae either, except in that game."

"What game?"

"A game all the cousins down here play and taught to all the cousins on Deddy's side, and taught to us, and Mama knows it, everybody knows it. Ella Mae is the ghost of a crazy woman who had drowned in Grandeddy's well after Granmama had helped deliver her born-dead baby. After she was found dead in the well, her ghost could be seen in the bathroom mirror at night, moaning for her baby."

"Child, what you talkin about?" She had shifted in the dirt and was looking down on me, squinting from the sun.

I went on, "It was supposed to be that if you went in the bathroom and turned off the lights and called her name over and over, she would come out and scratch you to death with her killer fingernails."

"Ain't that some shit. They can hide me the hell away and then make up somethin about what happened like I'm some kind of goddamn mythological bein."

She stood up and towered over me. "If you wanna come in here and eat some breakfast, I be glad to tell you exactly who I is and what is ghost story and what is just regular old tellin-the-truth story. Otherwise you can go on back and tell them Ella Mae ain't dead nor crazy as they think she is."

Despite the fact that she had given me an option, she picked up the Bible in one hand and grabbed me by the arm with the other. I was scared of the strength in her grip, but I wasn't scared of her. I didn't hear Granmama's voice in my head telling me to run.

24

Nothing Hid That Shall Not Be Manifested

Her house had wide-planked floors, just like the ones in Grandeddy's store. Sun beamed in from every window, and the walls still held some of the cool air from the night before. Plants in all kinds of odd-shaped pots, some giant and some just little clippings, lined the walls and hung in the windows. The air was peaceful and comfortable. The smell of smoked wood from her fireplace was caught up sweet and heavy in the air. Aside from the great room where I stood, there was her bedroom off to the left and a kitchen straight ahead.

She pulled up one of the wooden chairs that still had the bark of whatever tree it was made from. "Well, sit down. Don't stand there lookin like you ain't got no sense." I could tell she was still irritated about the ghost of Ella Mae.

The table was much too large for one woman, made of the same wood as the floor. It could seat ten easily.

I asked, "Does anybody else live with you? You have any kids or anything?"

"Nah. I do get a few people stoppin by every now and again. I can always hear them comin way off. Some of them buys a rug or two from me. I weaves my own rugs out of old coats, and shirts and all kinds of stuff other folk throw out."

"How come Mama and them don't talk about you? I never saw any pictures of you or anything."

"Folks bury the things they don't want to be lookin at inside they heads. They just find some kind of way to wipe it away or kill it so they can keep on surviving the best they can."

I looked down at the cup of tea she set in front of me and hid a grimace. Tea? I thought only white people drank tea, small dainty white women. I kept staring at the tea so I wouldn't see her reaction when I said, "Mama always changes stuff she doesn't want to think about. I mean, she doesn't want to deal with it. So it's like all of a sudden she goes from talking and laughing and being Mama, to not being able to see, or hear. Then all the craziness around her gets turned into one of her stories about the good times."

She laughed deep and so loud that her voice resonated in my chest. I smiled back at her, and she shook her head. "Lord, she done growed up and turned into Motha.

"I sho is glad to meet you, Odessa. You can tell me about my kinfolk, and I'll tell you about yours and sho-nuf we'll be talkin 'bout the same people." She laughed again and got up to go into the kitchen. "Drink your tea. It's got sassafras from down to the creek. Keep you from gettin dizzy till I can get some eggs fried up."

For a minute I forgot about Deddy hunting me. I forgot about Baby Jessie calling my name. I forgot about how every sip of tea, every inch that the sun crept higher, made my trouble with Mama and Deddy worse.

I never liked the way fried eggs smelled, thought they smelled too much like a wet chicken, but Elizabeth put onions in them. She said, "Cain't nobody expect a person with a good taste for food to just eat eggs dry-along-so."

When I was done and after I had eaten two pieces of homemade bread, I asked her if she would walk back to Grandeddy's house with me, maybe tell Mama that I had gotten lost.

"Child, I don't worry with them folks no more. You welcome to stay around here till you get your nerve up, but I ain't puttin myself in the way a none of them. They'll just find some way to get me mad and start talkin all kinds of stuff to make me want to hurt somebody.

"You ain't nowhere far from your Grandeddy's house, just head straight out there and cross over five barbed-wire fences, through that open field a rolled hay, back through them trees, and that's it. Ain't no more than a mile a two."

I got up and stood at her screen door, looking out as far as my eyes could see, and there was nothing that looked familiar. I couldn't even see another house from where I stood. Just some rows of corn off to one side, three cows in the distance, and a few groves of trees here and there.

"Elizabeth . . ."

"You ain't gotta call me that. Just call me Ella Mae. Long as you ain't plannin on talkin about me dyin in a well or scratchin somebody's eyes out, I ain't got no problem with you callin me that."

"Ella Mae . . . why does Mama and them pretend like you don't exist? And why do you live out here rather than just runnin away someplace far away from Grandeddy's house?"

"It's a long story, child. Life don't just unfold from a little question, 'How come?' Things happen the way they do by startin from long before a person is born, and by the time the wrongdoin get to you, it just pushes you to the way you is in this world, and you don't even know why."

I strained to understand what she was talking about and to connect it to my life. I didn't want to think that the things that Mama and Deddy did, the lies Mama told and the way Deddy tried to work my mind into a silent fear, were because of something before me that I couldn't fix.

"What was it like in the family when you were growing up?"

"You got to pick somethin for certain for me to tell you about. My mind ain't been just sittin around here waitin for you to show up so I can tell you thirty-somethin years' worth a livin."

"What happened for real, not the Ella Mae game, but the real stuff that somebody made it up from?"

She was sitting now in one of the chairs with her elbows on her knees, her hands clasped, looking me straight in the eyes. Her eyes clear, no shades pulled down behind them. She put her hair behind her ears, the hair that hung straight on either side of her head. Like Granmama's, it didn't look like black people's hair, and I wondered if she pressed it.

"I got weavin to do. Money don't make itself, and I got work to do on my plants, and some weedin out back. But I'm gonna take the time to tell you some things. But if there's any such thing that you already know to be the truth, just move me on along to save time."

"Yes, ma'am."

"Don't call me that, neither."

25

Moonshine

She pulled her chair in close. I was embarrassed that our knees almost touched, so I turned around in my chair and picked at the cold remains of my eggs and toast while she began her story.

"Well, first of all I'm the only child in my family that came out lookin different. Ain't nobody ever told me, but I know that my real deddy was a Indian man. I know it ain't supposed to be, but my deddy was my grandeddy, Motha's deddy.

"After Motha and Bo had already been married a long time, Motha's deddy used to come by and drank and carry on with Bo. Them and all the men that spent time at our house was plenty in good with the white men in Starkville.

"Bo and my Indian grandeddy had whiskey that ain't nobody else had, and Bo used to say you can sell a white folk anything he don't want if you can keep him drunk. Trouble was, Bo and my grandeddy was drunk pretty much too.

"Ain't nobody ever said it, but me and Motha look too much like my old Indian grandeddy. We lookin like sistas, not motha and daughter, and from my memory as a little gal I looks now like he look to me then.

"So ain't nobody ever said it, but me and Motha got the same deddy. After four children I was conceived right under Bo's nose. Older I got, round about five or six, more people starts saying how I sho-nuf ended up lookin like Motha and her Indian side more than I was lookin like Bo at all.

"I swear Bo started hating me right then, and any time he could find a reason to, he was tryin to tear the hide off of me. So everybody round these parts just start thinkin I was bad, because Motha said my Indian side made me mean. Right about then or thereabouts Bo and my Indian grandeddy started fightin all the time over whose money, and whose whiskey.

"I was just a child myself, but I knew too that they was fightin about how much my grandeddy treated me like I was his baby, not his granbaby. He called me Moonie 'cause he say I was his little Moonshine, and he took me with him every time he had a run to make.

"Motha didn't say nothin about it to neither one of them, just seem like more Bo hated my grandeddy, more she hated my grandeddy too, and more Bo hated me, more she ain't treated me right either.

"Yo mama, Bernice, and them wouldn't play with me except to tease me. And because when Bo would whup me I would fight back, Motha said I wasn't fit to go up to Ms. Bernadette house fo schoolin. Said if I didn't stop actin like a heathen, she was gone send me to the Choctaw reservation.

"Round about then there was some kind of commotion with some other Indian mens and Bo about my grandeddy's money, and I ain't never seen my grandeddy again since. I was about eight or nine, and ain't nobody ever talked about him eitha. Motha just let it go, just all the time said, 'God fix a sinner by and by.'

"Me, I like to got more badder than I already was with not having nobody to treat me special. Bo worked me right alongside Chet and Jo, said workin would get the Indian meanness out of me. Except all it did was made me strong as a boy. And that sho didn't seem to make nobody like me any better.

"I was from then on talkin 'bout how I was runnin off to Blackjack to ask folk if they seen my grandeddy."

I was lost in her story, building pictures in my mind. Somebody's voice other than Mama's was adding to my combination of memories and stories. "Did you ever get to Blackjack?"

"Sure I did. I never reached it on foot, but about the time I was fourteen, Bo started sendin me in the truck to deliver 'shine or pick up money for him. Motha used to tell him a girl didn't have no business doin stuff like that, but he just laughed and said I wasn't no girl, I was a heathen.

"I took every chance I had to ask anybody who even look like they was part Indian to tell me if they knew about my grandeddy. But mostly I was pickin white folks who had black hair and was not tellin nobody how come they look a little darker than most white folks. And more than one time I got into fights and Bo stop lettin me run his whiskey. Said I was bad for business. Seem like the colored people didn't want to be talkin about nothin like that, and the white folks was ready to hang me for bein a nigga who thought I was good enough to argue with white folks.

"Bo got in the habit of tellin me, 'Don't tell nobody that your dumb ass is kin to me. If they ask you, say you escaped off the reservation.'

"I reckon that's the best way to describe what you callin my childhood. But what probably causing your mama and them to be makin up tales about me bein some kind of ghost mournin for her child got somethin to do with stuff entirely different that I ain't sure you old enough or done built up enough doings in your life to be hearin."

I said, "I'm old enough. I've had to change diapers and take care of babies since I was nine. I have my period. . . ." I looked down at the floor and was a little embarrassed that I let that slip in my excitement.

She pulled one of the other chairs out from the table and said, "Sit down here. Now I'm tellin you this stuff so you'll know the real truth about all your people. Ain't nothin bein said for you to go runnin your mouth tellin people what you know. Besides if you old enough to be bleeding, you old enough to know what kinds a things this world can bring down on you now.

"I guess you can say I ain't never had nobody courting me like what you'd call a boyfriend. You got yourself a boyfriend yet?" She looked at me, concerned. I said back, embarrassed, "No."

"Ain't nothin to be ashamed of. You don't need to be ashamed of having one or not having one. Motha was always try'n to make me feel better about not having one by try'n to ask the sistas at church if they boys would take me along with your mama and them and they boyfriends when they was goin up to West Point to go to the color folks' dance house.

"But I ain't never liked to dance, and I didn't want to be bothered with no boys bein mad because I was stronger than them." We both laughed out loud. She seemed as pleased with my company as I was with hers.

"'Round about that time is when Bo started that mess about his own baseball team. Boys was comin from all over Mississippi to play on a team owned by a colored man. All the other owners was old white men who had gotten all they money the same way Bo did, from sellin 'shine back when our folks still couldn't get it.

"You should have seen your mama, Geraldine, Gladys, and Flora. When school let out, they would be servin drinks and standin around in all that dirt in they picture clothes, tryin to get them little old boys and grown men to look at them.

"Your deddy Loni and his brotha was in the young men that came up from Jackson."

I was a little surprised. "So Deddy and Leland really did play baseball?"

"That was his name, Leland. I ain't makin no mistake, am I?"

"That was his name. But he's dead now. He and Deddy had a fight, and Deddy ended up killing him."

Ella Mae shook her head, shocked at the news, shocked that I shared it so bluntly. "Lord have mercy. Trouble don't see its way out of this family."

We sat quiet for a while, Ella Mae contemplating Leland's death, then she went on.

"I ain't sayin they could play ball good, but they sho tried to work they way onto Bo's team. When there wasn't hardly enough men playin decent enough to lick any other teams, Bo made me play, and I didn't hardly mind. I liked playin ball betta than anything, and was the only one that could hit the ball out past the pasture and out to the big road."

She chuckled, shaking her head.

"Besides somewhat, I was glad Bo was actin like I was worth somethin. He told people my name was Jim Dandy. Jim was Bo's real name, but didn't nobody know that but Motha and us kids, and since my little tits didn't look like nothin under my jersey, and folks most the time thought I was a Indian man, then it worked out pretty good for everybody."

I thought it was a little strange that Granmama would let her girl play ball as a boy. "What did Granmama say? Did she say it was a good idea too, or did she not know about it?" I was hoping that maybe she was leaving out that Granmama didn't like what was happening.

She had said that Granmama said she was acting like a heathen—well, maybe Ella Mae was, but I just didn't think that Granmama would let Grandeddy make a boy out of one of her girls.

"Child, your granmama knew everything about anything that was happenin around her house. I ain't sayin you would have known that from her way of actin like she didn't know, but sho-nuf like your mama, she was deaf and blind when she wanted to be."

I looked away from her, out the window, where the wildflowers were climbing the vines on the outside of her house, their faces peeping in the windows. The sky was full of white clouds now, making the afternoon air thicker with humidity.

The two of us were quiet for a while, and I fought back tears. As much as I needed to be comforted, it didn't feel so good to have this woman who captured me with the curiosity of untold stories speak of Granmama like she was some heartless old woman when I knew she wasn't.

I closed my eyes to keep the tears from coming out. I was paralyzed in that chair. I couldn't move to go back to Grandeddy's, and I wasn't sure I wanted to sit there any longer pretending like I didn't have three little brothers I was going to miss terribly if I had to spend another night away from them. Everything was changing around me too fast. I should be with Towanda and Lamont. They wouldn't be with us next summer, and I knew that once they got to Mississippi State, they would look back at us Blackburns and be ashamed.

I forced my mind to stop dancing. "Can I have Granmama's Bible back? I'm gonna walk back to Grandeddy's house. I can figure out what to say on the way back."

Ella Mae seemed slighted. "Sho-nuf you can have it back. I ain't got no use for it. You the one asked me to tell you how things was." She got up and tugged on the bottom of her jean jacket to pull it away from the sweaty T-shirt that she wore underneath. "Well, you can quit lookin at me like that. If you's ready to go, you already know the way."

She reached across the table and gathered up the bulkiness of Granmama's Bible with her big hand. "I got things to do anyway. My whole day goin by the wayside messin around with you."

I felt guilty and said to her, finally letting the tears roll down, "I just wanna go home, okay?" I ran out and heard the screen door clap behind me. But I didn't head toward the barbed wire. Instead I cut away off to the right and ran with Granmama's Bible, black and sweaty in my hand. I could hear Ella Mae's deep voice, faint, calling after me, "Child, where you goin?" I wanted to be somewhere, not at

Grandeddy's, not with Ella Mae, so I could think. I had cried too many times in the past day. Too much confusion about everything.

I couldn't stand that someone who I only knew as a ghost was undoing my memories of my granmama, the one love I had understood all of my life.

26

Pallbearers

Ahead, I could see a tattered wooden building, and I stopped running. My overalls were covered with orange dirt, and I didn't look like I belonged to anybody.

After a few minutes of catching my breath, I dried my tears. Before me stood Granmama's church, the church that she used to take us to on summer Sundays, the church where her funeral had been. I never knew that it was walking distance from Grandeddy's house. I hadn't been there since that day, and though I remembered every minute of that day, Mama always said to me, "You ain't rememberin nothin from when you was only three years old, you just try'n to piece together stuff you done heard other people say." But that wasn't true, and I needed to prove that to myself.

As I walked up the wooden steps, I could see the brass, and the cherry wood of Granmama's casket on the shoulders of

black men in black suits, their steps keeping the rhythm of
tearful voices—Mama and the aunts, crooning.

> *Precious Lord*
> *Take my hand*
> *Lead me on*
> *Help me stand*

And other voices rose.

> *I am tired*
> *I am weak*
> *I am worn*

The pallbearers were Uncle Chet, Uncle Jo, Grandeddy, and
the woman who had taken me out of Mama's arms to the front
of the church to see Granmama in her casket, the woman with
big hands who had whispered into my small ear, "Don't you
never forget her face. You was her best granbaby. She tried to
love you because she couldn't love her own," the woman who
was Ella Mae.

I sat down on the steps and started to cry again. Why had I
been made to know all of this, to be the only one to meet Ella
Mae, to remember so sharply every wrong that had ever been
done to me? Maybe it was true. Maybe it was Granmama who
taught Mama how to be deaf and blind to what somebody was
doing to hurt her daughter.

In the distance I saw Ella Mae approach, and I tried to dry
my tears to make it look like I was wiping sweat. Her blue jean
jacket was finally gone, leaving her in a short-sleeved T-shirt
that hugged her muscular arms. Her steps were slow, rhythmic,
but wide. Each one brought her much faster than I expected.

She was black and Indian, and she did look wild. When I looked at her, I felt the same for her that I did for the Missouri tornadoes that we hid from in our basement, all of us too excited to be afraid. Mama told us to shut up so she could hear the wind. I imagined escaping the basement and running to the schoolyard, where the tornado came roaring and gutting everything in its path, and I would be afraid of losing my life but would sacrifice it to see something that awful and beautiful.

Ella Mae was awful and beautiful. I could feel her steps in my chest, her presence in the gut of my stomach. Feeling this, and knowing my mother, I knew how the Ella Mae story came about. She was different—her skin redder than Granmama's, her head large like a man's, and hair so dark it showed blue and green like a dragonfly's wings.

When she sat down next to me, I felt my heartbeat catch up with hers. "Child—one thing for sure, you as good a runner as I ever was. I would have brought you out here to this old church had you said that's where you wanted to go. Myself, I don't come around here except to tend Motha's grave. This place, they need to go on and knock it down. This is where your mama and them ought to be talkin about ghosts comin from. Sho-nuf, I'm tellin you."

Her face was shiny with sweat, and she was careful not to touch me. "Sorry if I got you upset about your granmama. I really ain't got no business tellin you certain things, whether you ask or not."

I yanked a whole handful of wild onions that were growing up high with the other weeds. "That's okay. I'm not any more upset knowing the family stuff that I didn't know than I am knowing all the stuff I've grown up with. I guess Mama and Deddy didn't get how they are by themselves, they must have learned it from someplace."

I pinched the end of the onions between my knees and started braiding them so I didn't have to look at her. "I've seen Deddy kill his own brother, I've seen Mama and Deddy try to kill each other, I been in Deddy's way more than once and got hit by a drunk fist."

I moistened my chapped lips. Giant tears fell out of my eyes and splashed on my onion braid. "I been done-it-to by Deddy . . . twice."

There was a long silence. She grabbed her own muscular arm like she was suddenly cold, and squinted up at the sky. She grunted, like someone had punched her in the gut. Then she looked at me like I was a map she couldn't make sense of.

She unfolded her rigid arms and put them around me.

I said, crying into the sweat of her solid chest, "I remember you taking me to the front of the church to see Granmama in her casket. I remember you telling me I was her favorite granbaby. But I didn't even understand who you were, and I didn't understand Granmama was dead."

Her heavy voice was more tenor now, watery. "Child, there's so much pain in this family. I wasn't supposed to even be at that funeral. Everybody act like it was my fault Motha was dead.

"I been hurt too, Odessa. Folks ain't supposed to be con-nected in the way I'm connected to people. Me and Motha having the same deddy, and me and you both been soiled by Loni."

I pushed away from her. I was dizzy from the heat, and tried to focus. *He did it to me, and Gretal, and Ella Mae.*

She grabbed my stiff body. Hot air swirled in the pit of my stomach, and I struggled to get out of her grip—"Let go. Please let me go"—but she wouldn't let go until I calmed down.

"I don't know what to tell you, child. All I can tell you is my own story. But I ain't even willin to tell that if you gone run off and treat me like a liar, like you did back at the house. I been having folks tell me I ain't nothin but a liar for the things I say all my life. I sho don't need that from you too. You cain't be cryin and fightin me, I ain't done you no harm."

27

Bone Teeth

The sun had come back out and was even hotter on its fall
toward early evening. She grabbed my hand and said,
"Come on to the back, where it's shady. If you ain't scared a
graves, I'll show you where some bodies lay."

Behind the church was a graveyard fenced in by a brick wall
only high to my thigh. A huge oak reached its limbs over the
graves. Its roots pushed the wall up in places, leaving crumbled
brick. Empty plastic flower baskets, satin ribbon, and the wire to
wreaths long since withered littered the small plot. In the shade
of the tree shiny grass had pushed up through last year's fallen
leaves. Some of the graves had wooden crosses, some stones
were made of poured cement, and a few were smooth granite
with machine-engraved letters. Granmama's was one of these.

Ella Mae bent down to dust the caterpillars off. "This is
where your granmama is buried."

The two of us stood on either side of Granmama's headstone. I spoke quietly over my granmama's grave. "I remember the burial. I can still smell the way the earth was, all dug up and damp when they lowered her casket."

Her stone read:

ELIZABETH LACEY
1914–1967
HE MAKETH ME TO LIE DOWN
IN THE GREEN PASTURES

Ella Mae pointed to a little grave that rested next to Granmama's. Stones mapped out the tiny plot.

"And this is my baby's grave. I don't really know where the body lies, though. When the baby died, Motha wouldn't tell me where they buried it. But when they stopped using this old church, I was sittin around here at Motha's grave, thinkin about how funny love is. You could love somebody who didn't hardly know how to be good to you, like I love Motha. And you could love somebody you only seen once, like I love my baby. That's because it mostly ain't about love, it's about needin folks to be what they supposed to be. This was supposed to be my mama."

Ella Mae pointed to Granmama's grave. "She was supposed to believe every word I say above somebody else." She pointed to the little mound. "And this supposed to be my baby. Don't make no difference how it had to come in this world, or who the daddy was, it was supposed to be my baby."

I asked her who the baby's father was. I wondered if Deddy made her pregnant.

"Loni," she answered. "Sho-nuf it ain't right, and I didn't expect no child to be born out of somebody hurting me. But that's the way it all come down."

I wasn't surprised, numb now to Deddy's sins. I asked her if she could tell me the rest of her story.

"I reckon I can tell you the rest, if you up to it."

"I want to know." I sat down and pulled weeds to keep from being too nervous.

She sat down, between the two graves, her legs stretching the length of Granmama's grave.

"Well, first of all Bernice and them was dead set on gettin either Loni or Leland to stop playin ball long enough to pay them some attention. Bernice was the first to make it, so she got Loni to start taking her to the colored folks' dance house every weekend. Leland was a different story. After the game he wasn't studying about hangin out with them gals. All he wanted was to be askin Bo this and that question about how to make white lightnin, and Bo kept him busy with wrong ingredients."

She stopped and started laughing. "I swear, Leland ended up makin everything from vinegar to rubbing alcohol.

"Neither one of them could play ball as good as me. Both of them talkin about how they was gonna get good and be the first colored men to join the St. Louis ball team. Said they'd be movin up to the city and comin back in a fancy car. Leland worked hard and got right good at ball after a while.

"Bo paid by the number of home runs you made, or number a times you struck somebody out, or caught a fly ball.

"I didn't get paid. Bo said, 'The roof over your head is your pay.'

"Afta while Leland got himself a old junky truck and said sho-nuf he had enough money to go on about his business to St. Louis. Your deddy liked to try to kill himself somebody. While he was messin around seein who he could make look at his muscles, Leland had done gone on and fixed himself to leave. He must have known just how your deddy would act, so he didn't tell nobody, just showed up for the ball game with his truck packed and his Sunday white shirt and good shoes and said, real city like, poppin on some chewin gum, 'I'm goin on to St. Louis. I don't have time to be messin around here in the dirt.' Then he turned to your deddy and your mama and said, 'Little brotha, when you can get out your own way, come look me up.' He pulled off, rocks and dirt makin a whole commotion while everybody just stared.

"Loni quit grinnin up in Bo's face then, kept sayin Bo had give Leland the money to go rather than him, and it didn't have nothin to do with the ball game. About that time, Loni tried to make like your mama was the only one he knew who could see what kind of 'good' he say he was.

"If it was one thing Bo didn't like, it was being called a liar or a cheat. He would say, 'Ain't a nigga gonna be caught dead callin me a liar.' He kicked Loni off the team, and a couple of times Loni came to the game anyway, drunk.

"Must have been your mama who told him I was really her sista Ella Mae, not some half-black Indian name Jim Dandy, because one day he showed up cussin Bo right in the middle of a winning game, embarrassin Bo in front of the other team owners. One of the men said, 'Cain't you control that nigga,' and Bo liked to got so mad at Loni that he ran, which he hated to do, back to the house and got his shotgun.

"About the time Bo got back, Loni had ran up to me and ripped my jersey open, showin my teats to them white men and everybody. He was shoutin, 'This motha-fuck been whuppin your teams with a Indian bitch. Look, teats and all!' I didn't even botha to button my shirt. I got my glove off and used these fists"—Ella Mae shook her fist over Granmama's grave—"and I tried to kill his ass.

"The game was forfeited. Bo went up to Loni and told him

he was lower than horseshit, and he didn't ever want to see his black ass around the ball field no more. Bo wasn't mad because Loni ripped my shirt open and showed everybody my business, he was mad because Loni made him out to be a cheat in front of them white men who he was in good with.

"That night Bernice was supposed to be goin with Loni to the end a high school dance in West Point. Far as Bo knew, she was gonna abide by what he said and go by herself, and he told me I had to take his good car and drive her. Well, I didn't hardly like that. I got into a big screamin fight with your mama, told her none a this would have happened had she kept her big mouth shut. But Bernice and Bo and everybody else was actin like it was my fault that Bo's team might go down for cheatin.

"Well, your mama got all dressed up in her party dress and white gloves and everything, and that was that. Motha said just go on and drive her and get it over with. She told me that when she was growin up she spent a lot a time arguing with her mother, and lookin back, she wish she had just done what she was supposed to do. She said it would've been easier.

"This didn't really satisfy me none, but Motha was the only one in the family who would show me in any kind of way that I was human. Even if it only was when nobody was lookin that she treated me right, it was still better than nothin. So when she said I ought to try and just not be makin Bo mad all the time, I always did try.

"There the two of us was, headin up the road. Bernice decided after a while to tell me that she wanted me to drop her off up near Ms. Bernadette's old schoolhouse because she was meetin Loni there. And I just let her talk, and didn't even look over at her. There I was in a old T-shirt and work pants because that's all I had to wear. Last new thing anybody had bought for me was my baseball shirt, and that no-good bastard had tore that open and made me to be like somethin from the carnival.

"Your mama was gettin treated like she wasn't no kin to me, gettin chauffeured around in Bo's car that he ain't never before that day let me lean on let alone drive.

"We was approachin Ms. Bernadette's old schoolhouse that had been vacant for five years, and closer we got, I could see Loni standin there leanin against his old raggedy truck, just waitin for me to do what the two a them thought I was s'posed to do. Nobody ever had any consideration for my feelins whatsoever.

"I was really just plannin on scarin him and keeping on down the road to West Point where I was supposed to be taking Bernice. But that ain't what happened. I swear I go to do one thing, and look like to me the situation always get worse."

She was looking out past my head at the fields. Her eyes were heavy with pain, and red from holding back tears. I was ashamed now. And I knew that whatever else there was to the story, Ella Mae had been made to suffer for lots of stuff that other people had done wrong. I knew that Mama and Deddy, and Granmama and Grandeddy, had just taken whatever they didn't want of the past and heaped it on Ella Mae.

She took a deep breath, tucked her hair behind her ears, and started up again. "Well, I swerved to play like I was gonna hit him, and my wheels stuck in the water ditch on the side of the road. I went a few yards tryin to get the tires to catch back up on the road, but it was too late. I ran headlong into a tree. About the time I came to, I felt like somebody had took a sledgehammer to my ribs. Glass was everywhere, and Bernice wasn't even in the car. She was laid out in the field with Loni cryin over her. To hear that man cryin was somethin pitiful. Sounded like a cow gettin branded."

We both laughed a little. "I managed myself out the car and we got Bernice into the back of Loni's truck. We drove straight to the hospital in West Point. Yo mama had a concussion, glass stuck in her face, mostly her forehead, and a missin tooth. All and all, she wasn't too bad off considerin. The doctor checked me for broken ribs but they was just big bruises from the steerin wheel.

"Afta that day the real things that happened with the accident was me and Bernice and Loni's secret, 'cause Bernice didn't want Bo to know she had gone behind his back. Bernice and Loni claimed I was jealous of the two of them being together, and said that I wanted Bernice lookin toothless with her face all scarred up.

"Wasn't no use tryin to tell Bernice it was a accident, that I just was gonna scare him a little. Bernice sat up in that hospital and said to me, 'You gonna have to do a whole lot more than that to take away my God-given beauty. I swear before God and anybody else who can hear me, I'll rot in hell before I see your heathen ass have any kind of a boyfriend.' I told her it didn't make me no never mind. Wasn't nothin I was gonna do with no man that I couldn't do for myself. She took that to mean I didn't need no man to satisfy my urges. You should have seen the way her face twisted up like she smelled a skunk lettin loose or somethin.

"Yo mama always did have a real smooth beautiful round face, and only time I ever thought she was ugly was when she sat there with that bandage around her forehead and looked at me like I stunk.

"She said back to me that I better stay away from her and her sisters and all they girlfriends. That ain't nobody 'funny' gonna be callin herself kin to her. She say she hated me and couldn't stand lookin at my weird ass. I guess that's why she didn't show one bit of mercy for me when Bo saw what I did to his new car. He picked up one of his baseball bats and cracked me up beside the head.

"Motha let me rest my head in her lap while she used her own needle and thread to stitch my skin together. She said to me, 'I told you about drinkin Bo's liquor!' She held my head still, and started yellin this over and over. And it was obvious to me, since she knew that I wouldn't never drank nothin made by Bo's hands, that she was screamin for all her own sins and just usin words that seem to fit Bo's satisfaction.

"That whole next week went by, and Bernice came home from the hospital with a bandage still over her forehead. Everybody hovered over her, all the sisters and brothers waitin on her hand and foot. Her, Geraldine, Gladys, and Flora like to constantly be huddled up whisperin somethin then lookin at me like I was crazy when I walked by. You would have thought the way they kept me away from Baby Sis, that's your Aunt Nell, that I was gonna eat her up or somethin.

"And Bernice, she ain't wanted nobody that wasn't kin lookin at her toothless mouth. Bo bragged about how he was gonna take her to get a gold tooth to replace what had been took away.

"When they went for her tooth, there was all kinds of showin out by her. Motha did her hair all around the bandage, and she got dressed up in the party dress from the accident. Motha spent three or four days at the washtub fixin it.

"On the way back from gettin her tooth, Bernice made Bo stop by the fillin station and take her picture in front of his crumpled-up car.

"I ain't never seen no need for somebody to be walkin around with gold sittin up in they mouth, but Bo sho did like tellin folks that he replaced his child's bone tooth with a gold one.

"I didn't have much need to be hangin around the house no more. Didn't seem like nobody like me, never did, and it seem like Motha was just turnin inward on herself—sewin or cookin or fussin over Bernice and them who was talkin about gettin married and goin up North.

"Time passed, winter came and all, and didn't nobody seem to take notice that Loni was comin back around for Bernice. Look like Bo just forgot about what he was mad about, and look like the white men for the other teams forgot too, because come spring they was all back out behind the store playin ball and drinkin. Loni and Bo was all of a sudden like best friends. Look like Loni was gettin smart enough to know who to be good to and how to keep his mouth shut when Bo was talkin."

28

Omens

Over the years Mama, Deddy, Grandeddy, and all my aunts and uncles had begun to dry up like the apple-head dolls we made from leftover Christmas apples. But in Ella Mae's story, they were like characters in the soap operas.

The sun beamed down heavy on the spot where we sat and heated up the plastic flowers, leaving a dry odor that reminded me that I was thirsty and hungry. Ella Mae looked at me with her hand shielding the sun and pulled a Slim Jim from her back pocket.

"You hungry?"

I forced myself not to hesitate in answering yes. Until this moment, I hated beef jerky like I hated sardines and Spam; all the foods that made my parents seem country. Ella Mae broke it in half and finished her story.

"Afta while, Loni and Bernice got married and moved on

up to St. Louis and start having babies. Motha act like she was more proud of that than anything, and start sendin Nell up with Geraldine, Flora, and Gladys to visit your mama. Then after a while they was talkin about gettin they stuff and movin too.

"Our house felt bare right fast with nobody left but me and Jo and Chet. And I just as soon been invisible anyway, because didn't nobody treat me like I was no kind of good. Seem like as long as all the sisters and brothers was livin in the house, then the bad stuff didn't seem to have no hold in my mind. But after a couple of years a livin in that house with most everybody gone, I ain't wanted nothin to do with bein in a place that made me feel so bad. Seem the more quiet it was around there, the more I could remember Bo and my grandeddy fightin, and Bo beatin me with a stick or whatever he could get his hands on.

"I took to sleepin up there on that little piece of land that Bo had stole. From what Motha told me, he schemed the only other colored bootlegger out of his piece of land back when they was young.

"When I first started comin up here, I made a little old wood tent no higher than my knee. That year I like to froze to death, and every now and then I'd go sleep up in Motha's kitchen at night and leave right early before anybody woke up. When it got spring again, I start bringin Bo's tools and things up here to build me my house. First I tried to only take stuff he wouldn't miss and then put it back quick. But afta while it was clear enough for me that he and Motha act like they didn't know what I was doin because they wanted me gone anyway. Look like soon as I wasn't livin there no more, all the sisters and brothers start comin home in the summertime and bringin they kids for Motha to see them grow. I sometimes watch all the little ones play, me lookin from out behind the trees just to see what everybody look like.

"Things went on like that for a couple of years while I build my house.

"One night before I had the roof on yet, I lay there on my floor lookin up at the sky, thinkin about how I don't care nothin about bein by myself, how folks supposed to want to be with they people, how womens supposed to want to be married, but I ain't never cared about none of that. I laid there on my own floor made from the trees that used to stand there and I looked up at the stars lookin like dust over my head, and me the only woman I knew who was like a heathen, a animal. I laid there thinkin 'bout everythang.

"I was already twenty-somethin years old. I knew that this world—Motha, Bo, my sisters and brothers, my Indian grandeddy, them dead trees that was now my floor, and all the stars above my head—didn't have nothin to do with no God. Things just was the way they was, ugly or beautiful, and me or nobody else didn't have no control over prayin for none of it to be different.

"I fell asleep just thinkin like that." Ella Mae paused and looked up at the sky. "I was woked up in the middle of the night by your deddy."

Her face didn't change, it was desolate, but one tear rolled out of her eye, leaving a trail of moisture over her weathered cheek.

"Somebody had give him a gun. He knew that even if he took me by surprise, I would've killed him with my bare hands if it wasn't for that gun, a gun just big enough to fit in one hand. Ain't no way he would've been able to do to me what he did. When he was on top a me he said he was gonna show me what I needed a man for. Said maybe I could do *almost* everything a man could do."

I could see Deddy, a smoother, thinner man than the one who cut the fur from the rabbit's ankles.

Ella Mae went on, "And when he was through holdin that gun to my head, he hit me with the butt end of it. My ears filled with a hissin noise, and I laid there knocked out, dreamin about tryin to climb up over side of a bridge. That bridge was on fire, and I ain't never forgot that dream.

"When I woke up, it took me a minute or two to separate my dream from what had happened. But when I did, I pulled up my work pants, blood and all, and ran outside and grabbed the ax I had stuck in a tree trunk. I ran out across the fields after him.

"The light of the morning was in the sky, but there wasn't no sun rise yet, just me barefoot and dark hair. I don't remember my feet on the ground, just the feel of that ax in my right hand, held high like a torch."

I could see her running. Her hair and the ax like an omen coming on fast, her face solid, fierce, her breath escaping with each beat of her feet on the earth. I was crying now and trying to stay quiet so Ella Mae would keep talking. I needed now to know everything that had been said and done. I didn't let myself doubt her anymore. She had no reason to lie.

All my life I had to believe Mama's stories, even the ones where I had been present. Mama painted over my images, daring me to contradict her. Now someone else was painting on me, someone I trusted because she was letting me know how she too had been hurt.

She went on telling. "I couldn't see nothin but red, and everything I had ever been mad about, everything that sat around inside my chest waiting for change, it all tried to take itself out in the swing of my ax. Everybody in Bo's house looked like my enemy. I was scared and angry, like I had the rabies, and they all looked evil to me. I moved grown folks with that ax. Motha, Bo, Jo, and Chet, all moved out the way of my swing. I screamed for Loni to come out, but he wasn't nowhere to be found. Bo and Jo finally snuck up behind and grabbed me and pulled me to the ground. I was screamin even after they dragged me out to Motha's room and give me five a six glasses a whiskey.

"I reckon that's what you could call the first one of them fits they say the devil put in me. But nobody would listen to the real cause of them, how somewhere in my heart"—Ella Mae was sweating again and had her arms folded tight, like she was cold—"somewhere in my heart, I knew that everything about my life was wrong—didn't nobody have no business treatin me like the folks call themselves my kin was treatin me.

"Tellin my story sho-nuf makin me remember things that I didn't even know I made myself forget. I sho-nuf always knew my own story, but till I hear it comin cross my lips, it make me see that things was even more awful than I thought they was."

29

The House of the Lord

Ella Mae turned to look me in the eyes, but I looked down at
the little mound of earth. She talked more, still looking in
my direction. "I'm thinkin about you bein hurt and how you
was strong. You sho got me feelin ashamed a keeping my
mouth shut all this time."

She looked at me, exhausted, and I could see how reliving
her past had aged her.

"Now what I tell you on the rest of this, you just got to
know that some people's weaker than they want to admit. And
life, it just keep on movin whether you come along with it or
not. So sometimes people do what feel like is gonna make
things better for right then. They don't bother to think about
what the turnin of the years gonna bring. All they got the
strength to think about is what's gonna feel better for a short
while.

"When I lay there in Motha's bed tryin to remember where my ax was, listn'n to Motha say over and over, 'Say your name. Say your name,' I knew that she was healin me back from someplace she herself had been before. She took my hand and laid it on the squares of that old patchwork quilt on her bed and said what all the pieces a clothes were before they was quilt. She say my grandeddy name over and over to remind me of somebody who I loved in this world. She brought me back. And when my face let go of madness, I cried, and when I cried, she got up and closed the door.

"That's when I said to her, clear, 'Loni soiled me.' I told her that he opened up my body where only your husband supposed to touch you. When I say that, she finished the job a taking me away from that pain by giving me another sip a white lightnin, and kissin my forehead like I was her baby again.

"Then she said to me, 'Loni and Bernice and them kids left here yesterday. Now you know ain't he or nobody else been up to where you stayin. You know better than to say that. You got to let the devil stop having your soul. On Sunday you gonna go get baptized down at the river.'

"About then, I looked in her eyes and knew that she done lied to me and herself, and I knew she wasn't gonna be able to love me no more."

Till now the sky had seemed eternally bright, but with Ella Mae's last words the sky dropped its light, and I felt myself get heavy with grief for all that was gained and lost in the past two days.

Granmama had not protected Ella Mae. Mama had not protected me. And when we tried to speak, we had been fed homemade rum cough syrup or white lightning as a cure. I was sick in my stomach now. How we must have looked—a mammoth woman, young but old, and me, grown tall, my overalls two days dirty, my hair still in two French braids, nappy from sweat, both of our eyes swollen from tears cried over Granmama's grave.

I reached into my back pocket to get Granmama's Bible. It didn't feel the same in my hands as it had a summer ago.

I asked Ella Mae what Gretal had asked me, "Do you believe in God?"

"I ain't got no use in believin in God. Some folks gets a great deal of peace in this world by believin in God—prayin and carryin on—but ain't nothin ever come good to me by talkin about what God gonna do, or what the next world gonna be like.

"I never did get baptized, because I had started the mornin sickness and Motha knew I was pregnant from what Loni done to me, and when she knew that, she said wasn't no use in me gettin baptized now, it wasn't gonna do me no good.

"Way I see it, God and me just wasn't never meant for each other. Seem that he ain't had room in his kingdom for a pregnant woman and a bastard child less it be by his own doin."

I wanted to know the rest now. "So your baby died?"

"I stayed out here fixin my house. I finished the roof before I even got big, and wasn't nothin left to do but tend to it all, and make it look like somethin. Motha started bringin me this and that, and just leaving things on the porch if I was sleep with weakness from growin a baby, or she would just come by, say, 'How you makin out? This just somethin I was bringin by,' and go on 'bout her business without stayin long enough for me to ask her anything, or make any kind of conversation.

"She brought plant clippings from her garden, seeds, and

one mornin, a little old wooden loom she used to keep in the shed. Her note on it said 'MAKE YOUR BABY SOME BLANKETS TO STAY WARM.' But she ain't give me nothin to make it with, so I start taking all the rags and work clothes I couldn't hardly fit in and made what I called rugs, because sho-nuf they was too rough to be blankets."

She laughed. Her face had softened with the telling of the coming of her baby.

"I reckon the longer I was pregnant, the more I didn't care nothin about how that baby got in me. I just kept seein me and my baby livin in the house I built. Growin flowers, playin, me loving my baby the way it feel good to have somebody love you, like you the only one in the world can make them happy."

30

The Ghost of Ella Mae

The night my water broke, my pain came down hard every few minutes. I ain't never felt nothin like that before in my life. Much as I thought I was gonna be having that baby like the cow have her baby calf—just let it come on out, then clean it up and nurse it—all I could think was, 'Motha, help me!'

"My mind wasn't workin on nothin in that kind of pain except gettin to my motha. These fields turned into a space as big as the world. All I could take was a few steps, then I was down on my knees beggin the crickets and things to shut up so I could concentrate on not dyin. I begged the night sky to give me the moon or the stars or somethin to wish on, somethin besides that heavy black sky that pushed down on me.

"When I got there, Geraldine had brought Baby Sis Nell down to visit Motha, but the two of them ain't done nothin to help. Geraldine acted like I was too nasty to touch, and

Baby Sis ain't never knew no betta than to be scared of me.

"Motha got me in the tub and rubbed my belly with the warm water I was squattin in. Everything was turnin round in my head. I was sweatin and thinkin about how to do what Motha say so the baby would come out all right. I was lookin in Motha's eyes, and she was tellin me to push, but I could feel somethin evil in her, evil with shame. Somehow, I could feel her wishin the baby be dead, harder than I was wishing it be live.

"I started screamin for my baby. We was screamin and carryin on somethin awful, and before I passed out, my baby came out into the water, blood and life squirmin and reachin for to get out of all that slime and into its mama's arms. In my weakness I couldn't come all the way to. It was like somethin thick and heavy was holdin me in to my sleep, but sho-nuf I could hear my baby cry.

"When I woke up, Motha and Bo, Geraldine, Nell, Jo, and Chet all stood over me where I was layin in Motha's bed. They was lookin at me like I was dead. Motha say, 'Your baby died. Lord have mercy, it done gone on to glory.' She started right up to cryin, but I ain't said nothin, just laid there and stared, because I knew somethin wasn't right.

"I could tell by the way Motha smelled like fear, by the way she looked down on me. I could tell, because my shirt was just wet with milk for my baby.

"I said back to her, real calm like, 'Bring me my baby.' She answered back, cryin harder, 'You cain't be actin up now, your baby was born still.'

"I couldn't stand to see Motha cry, but for the first time I didn't feel a twist in my belly when I looked at her this way. I could just remember the sound of my baby's cryin, and I asked her again, loud this time, 'Where my baby!' I didn't care that Bo and them was lookin at me and shakin they heads. Nell ran out the room like she was scared a bomb was gonna go off. Nobody answered me. I looked at all of them, and nobody said a word, till Geraldine looked down on me with them glasses of hers, examining me, and said, 'She ain't gonna be good for nothin now.'

"Heat rolled over me. I could feel myself bein raised up out that bed, moving my feet and fists through walls, bringing the whole house down with the strength of my voice."

Ella Mae talked now like she was preaching. "Nothin was mine in this world. Motha and them wasn't gonna even let me have my baby. They had done killed it or let it die. Ain't nothin was mine no matter what I did. Nothin in this world I could make real, and I understood that right then. I could see myself tearin Motha's house to pieces, and Bo and Chet and Jo chasin me like I was a hornet loose in the house, laughin like it was some kind of game."

She paused to catch her breath and looked up at the sky to see where the sun had gone. Even though it was still light out and very hot, the day had floated over us.

Her voice fell to a whisper, "I don't know what happened to me, but for a long while after that night, I walked in my sleep and went back to the house on occasion lookin for my baby. I reckon that's how that crazy game a yours got started."

><

I wanted to believe that I had always known her, because I felt now like I always had, and I trusted her more than anybody.

"Did you ever have any fits when I was little? Did you ever come around when we visited Grandeddy?"

"I seen y'all kids of Bernice's at the funeral, and I seen you some before and afta then. But I ain't never had no fit when y'all was down here. And I ain't had no fit since Motha died."

She got up from Granmama's grave, but her eyes stayed focused on the mound of dirt. I stood up too, and we both dusted off. She looked down to where I left the Bible. "Don't leave that there. Neither one of us might not have no use for them words in it, but it belonged to your Granmama, and I knew how she treated you like you was somethin special. And far as I know ain't nobody let you have nothin that belonged to her, so you might as well have them pictures and that old book she put all her loving in."

Exhausted, she said, "I reckon I don't know where we walkin to now, back to my house or to Bo's, but we best start on our way."

We headed out of the graveyard. I stepped over the high weeds that only came to Ella Mae's knees. As we passed the church, I etched into my memory its broken windows and puckered boards.

31

Flesh of My Flesh, Blood of My Blood

Our smells were thick in the humid air, mixed with the sweetness of hay and cow manure, both of our odors sharp. We walked slow now, side by side, retracing where we had torn through the grass earlier that day.

Her voice came slow and rhythmic like our walking. "I'm gonna go on and tell you all the rest there is to tell, because my life and your life sho-nuf is tied together by the same wrong-doin.

"For everybody else, life just went on after that. Your mama kept on bringing new babies down here every summer, Chet moved on up to St. Louis to be with the rest of them, Jo went on and married that gal he got pregnant from down the road. When they had that retarded baby, Bo helped Jo build them a house on the property.

"For me and Motha things wasn't never gonna be right

after I lost my baby. I went on ahead and put Motha in the same place in my heart where I kept everybody else who I didn't have no use for. That don't mean her and I ain't never talked again, but sho-nuf wasn't no hope of it even bein like it was before. She didn't even see fit to comfort me when wasn't nobody lookin, and I didn't even care no more. I just stayed out here, livin my life like there ain't never was no family that I had.

"In my head, my Indian grandeddy was the only one on earth I ever had, and he was the only person on the earth I ever know'd. I knew in my heart, even inside my house, that I couldn't really kill the truth. Couldn't kill it because no matter what, every year spring come, then the beginning of summer, and all my ghosts in my head come back to me. I tried to lock myself inside my own house at night when I knew the time a year was comin that my baby was lost from me. But once or twice, I manage to get out of my house, and when I woke up, I was on the floor with Bo threatening to kill my crazy ass if I didn't get out of his house.

"The last time I threw a sleepwalkin fit, I come over the field at night, 'sleep, but runnin with fire and death in my eyes. I woke up with my hands around Motha's throat. Bo was out drinkin, and Jo and his wife and his little retarded boy lived too far down the road to hear me screamin at Motha or to hear Motha screamin for her life.

"In her eyes I saw her death and mine, I saw a pit deeper than hell where she had buried my baby. Afta while, I know'd I was awake, but I didn't let go of her throat because I knew I had things to say that I ain't never had the nerve to say when I was awake."

Ella Mae picked up her walking pace, and I worked hard now to keep up with her and keep the space between us short for better listening.

"Sometimes folks just don't think about what they doin, they just thinkin about what be the best thing at the time. We all done made them kind of mistakes before. Motha, me—" Ella Mae looked down to make sure that she caught my eyes in her glance. "I'm sure even you done did stuff you ain't hardly give yourself a chance to think about.

"I said it all to Motha right then, 'You ain't never loved me. I know'd we was born into this world by the same man. I know we got the same deddy. I know you done somethin to my baby. I know! I know!'"

She talked now like she was there again and I longed to see her face and know that she was not having one of her fits. "I just kept on like that for a long time, even though I wasn't hardly squeezin her neck no more. And she was just a cryin, lettin all the gumption go out of her. She wasn't even yelling at me no more, just layin there limp. And she say back sobbin, 'I done did the best I could. I been scared in this world too. There's pains I live with every day that you don't know nothin about. I try to send your baby away out of this life that I been livin, out of this life you been livin. Ain't no use for me no more. It was the best thing to do to leave you where the devil had already took you, and to do what was best for your child.'

"About now she was all out of tears and all out of words. I knew she knew I wasn't sleepwalkin no more. And I let go of her, and I was ashamed of myself—her layin there curled up on the floor like she wasn't hardly nobody's mama, and me sittin there after tryin to kill her. We was just a mess.

"Next mornin I lay quiet in my house, flipping things over in my mind—ponderin on leavin, but 'fraid to go out there beyond this land, ponderin on stayin, but not knowin how I can be here waiting for the love of a woman who took my only thing in this world away from me. I heard somethin rising up out of the fields before daybreak. Sound like a flock of geese cryin through the damp air. I walked one step at a time through the fields away from my house, knowin inside the meat of my bones that these fields wasn't never gone look the same to me again. When I got to Motha's house, Bo had lifted her out the bathtub and laid her on the floor. Her face wasn't red or pink with living, but gray like pickled pigs' feet. Wasn't no blood left in her after she had laid down in the tub and cut her own neck with the knife she used to clean chickens with. That old Bible and all them photographs was laid out on the floor.

"I moved through the room like a invisible woman denying myself grief or upset. Ain't nobody seen me, because Bo and Jo and his wife was screamin and cryin about needin to call this one and that one, screamin for God to help. I just picked Motha's things off that dirty floor, put them all together with a rubber band, and walked in her room and put them in her night drawer where they belonged. Then I walked on home, not cryin, not feelin nothin."

I felt the life drain out of my body, and a knot grew in my stomach at the thought of Ella Mae being cold and heartless the way my own mother could be. I choked back nausea at the image of Granmama limp and gray, all of her blood and life gone, a thin film of red on the bottom of the tub where I had poured many pans of hot water to bathe myself and my little brothers.

Me and Ella Mae just stood, staring now. Her house emerged in the distance, the light of the sky going soft and leaving the house and the crape myrtle tree as black silhouettes.

Ella Mae spoke into the silence. "I walked back to my house and just waited day and night, walkin up to the edge of Bo's property and peepin through the trees to see your mama and y'all and all the folks comin down here for the funeral. Sho-nuf when the time come, I took the only dress I still had from my old church clothes and dyed it black with pokeberries and walked across this same path to bring myself to the funeral, where I knew didn't nobody want me to be."

I could hear Granmama singing in the waning light of the field behind us; her spirit had always spoken forewarning to me. *He'll come back with your blood,* but now she moaned, quiet, as darkness rose up over her grave and swallowed the fields we'd jouneyed through. I thought about Ella Mae's words, "Sometime people do what feel like it's gonna make things better for right then. They don't bother to think about what the turnin of the years gonna bring."

Her words didn't seem to do any good for the loss I felt. Granmama sacrificed her life, took a knife to her own body as punishment for her sins against Ella Mae.

"Why did you say those things to her?" I asked, reaching out, catching Ella Mae's damp, sweaty T-shirt.

She stopped and looked up at the sky, but did not turn around. "It was time I spoke," she whispered.

I picked the dry skin on my lip, trying not to slip into anger or pity or tears. I needed to be thinking, not crying. My head hurt now, and I wanted to be back at Grandeddy's so I could see all the floors and walls of his house and know that now, the meaning of every crack and dent and warped floorboard would be changed. I wanted to see and feel my mama's life. I wanted to see her young face in the photographs, and put the reality of Ella Mae's life into Mama's blank eyes. I wanted to see again the place where I spent so many summers, to go back and remember myself standing barefoot, knowing that beneath my feet, many years of a missing aunt's blood, and my granmama's blood, had been washed away.

Ella Mae interrupted my thoughts. "I reckon there ain't nothin else that you don't remember for yourself. Just, I know'd you was Bernice's child when I saw you in the hay, because every now and then, about this time a evening in the summer, I come to the edge of Bo's property and watch y'all kids play. Sho-nuf y'all bigger every year." Her voice had stayed in a low whisper of shame.

"This time I guess the world see fit for me to stumble on you in the dark. And I suppose it ain't right that I didn't just make you go on back to Bo's, but I knew if you was lying about where you come from, then somethin wasn't right with you. Recently when you come down here, you keep to yourself, not like how you was at the funeral, all hugged up against everybody."

And I remembered Mama's arms around me on the front pew at the church. It was the last time she pulled me close to her. I looked at Ella Mae and remembered Mama reaching and Ella Mae scooping me up.

"Mama is always mad at me, all the time." I was looking at the ground now. I couldn't look at Ella Mae's back anymore; my face still showed a big bruise beneath my glasses. We had been talking about her life, forgetting about the trouble I was in. I couldn't catch my breath when I thought about what would happen when I got back. I felt dizzy with hunger and anguish. My feet shifted in discomfort, and the red cracked earth gave way beneath me.

Ella Mae turned to me and almost laid her hand on my shoulder to comfort me, but I shrank away and curled myself closer to the ground. I wished I was beneath the dirt, silent, at peace, no more pain, and I screamed into my dirty hands. "I can't go home, I can't stay here. I want to die. I want to die."

Ella Mae exhaled a deep breath as if she had been punched

in the gut, and before I could look up, her thick arms were around me. She lifted me and covered ground quickly with her stride. I struggled to get out of her grip, but she pinned me close to her chest, the smell of her sweat like mildewed leather. Her heart beat frantically, and for the first time since our voices met in the darkness, I was afraid. In my mind I saw the glowing green eyes, the long killer fingernails, and frayed hair that Gretal had seen in the mirror.

"Be still, be still, chile. Ain't nothin in life ever just took care of itself. It be about time I did somethin right. Ain't nobody else gone be dead on account of the mens in this family, nobody else."

I bit my own tongue, and the rhythm of her steps distracted my tragic thoughts. She stopped walking and put me down, unfolded me, and stood me up in the place where we had met. The rolls of hay and our two figures were outlined by the blue night sky. The last band of peach light fell beneath the trees and beyond Grandeddy's house.

"You listen to me. You's a chile. You ain't got no business wishin to be dead."

She put her rough hands on my cheeks and looked me in the eyes the way Miss Clay did whenever she saw me walking with my head down.

"Wishin 'bout bein dead and wishin to be invisible like I do all the time is 'cause you don't feel like you can do somethin about the way things is. But it's gotta stop, Odessa, it's gotta stop." Her voice was shaky, and I strained to see if she was crying. "Now let's go on and do what need to be done."

I pulled against her. "What needs to be done?" I remembered running through the school yard in my dream, trying to reach Deddy before he was dead. "Ella Mae? Wait. I don't want . . . I don't want . . ."

"Stop cry'n now and come on. I ain't crazy. I ain't havin no fit. I just understand somethin 'bout my life now." She grabbed my hand to bring me with her. Fear welled up inside me like soda swallowed too fast, up my throat, into my head, my nostrils burning. We picked up speed, almost running, ready to have so many things done with. The trees rushed past, and a whippoorwill called out to the setting sun.

When we got to the eleven trees, my head felt swollen with the facts of my own life, and I couldn't think. It was all happening too fast. Even the darkness had come on so fast that my eyes adjusted slowly. And there he was, Deddy sitting in Granmama's old rocking chair, waiting under the light. A cloud of moths and mosquitoes swarmed above his head. The house behind him was dark and quiet without the sound of kids' voices. Our van sat silent, waiting, an ominous foreshadowing of my capture.

I heard the voices inside me scream, like an alarm that had gone off. And I remembered again my dream, Deddy calling me through the woods to Granmama's porch—"Get a bucket and wash all this blood off the walls."

I held on to my knees, sweating, looking up at him, then over at Ella Mae, who stood tall as one of the trees. Her hair was dark like the night, and her eyes were fixed like a dog on its prey.

Ella Mae and I moved up the steps of the porch, silent like storm clouds. When we got to the top step, Deddy stopped rocking, and I stepped down to put distance between us. The porch light showed the thinness of the hairs on the crown of his head—specks of gray in his short Afro. He stood up; his white shirt tucked in, his stomach slightly hanging over the waist of his slacks. He walked to the edge of the porch, his heels knocking on the weathered boards. Like a young man, he leaned with one arm high on the beam, and smirked, then let loose a laugh, amused at the sight of me and Ella Mae.

He struggled to get himself together. "Ain't this some shit. You call yourself runnin away from here, and you run to one fucked-up motha-fucka. I guess you had one night of her and found out she was 'funny,' and here you come back. I figured you be back. Your ass ain't too crazy. You know the difference between when you got it good, and livin in some old bug-infested, raggedy-ass log cabin with somebody who's fuckin crazy."

He was still smirking and grinning. Ella Mae and I stood solid. I looked up at him and asked with my teeth tight together, "Where is Mama and them?" He laughed again.

"You done missed your callin. Ain't nobody waited around here for two days for your ass to decide to come back. Hell, don't nobody give a damn about you runnin off into the woods. Me and Bernice figured you was up there to her house anyway. Your mama ain't had enough backbone to carry her ass up there and get you, but just like I told her, you'd come right back here."

While he worked on unbuckling his belt, he talked to me and Ella Mae like we were both his children. "Now you, 'Dessa, is gonna get your ass whipped, then we gettin on the road. And you, Miss Jim Dandy, gonna carry your hermit ass back up in the woods, and think about stayin the hell out of my business."

The two of us still hadn't moved. It was like Deddy was onstage. I didn't know what else to say but the truth. "No, thank you. I think I'll stay here with the hermit." His head moved back in exaggerated surprise. I concentrated on not shrinking back from my own words.

"You think that shit is funny?" His belt bridged the space between us. Without warning, the leather strap came whipping through the darkness and slashed across my face breaking my unyielding stare.

In the time that it took me to reach up to calm the sting on my cheek, Ella Mae lunged from where she stood. She came down on Deddy with her whole body. Their weight boomed on the decaying porch, a hollow sound that brought back the sound of me and Deddy's bodies slamming to the floor in the sitting space. Air escaped from my lungs.

Ella Mae's voice was deep like thunder. "Don't you ever touch her again. I ain't gonna never let it happen that you gonna ever touch nobody again."

She slammed his head to the floor of the porch, and the images of Uncle Leland's murder washed over me, and my body stiffened with a premonition of black dresses, and chrome handles on dark wood, satin lining. I reached for my ears, but their bodies were still slamming against the porch floor. I didn't want him dead, I didn't think I wanted him dead.

Deddy rolled over and got his handgun out of the back of his pants.

Time slowed, the air thickened, Ella Mae rolled over to get up. She moved way too slow to catch up with Deddy's palm around the gun handle, his finger working with his perfect vision to pinpoint his hunt.

It was hard to stay, not stiffen to a hard plank and stand silent and dead until the confusion steadied itself into my next grieving. And out of the darkness, leaning against the porch, Granmama's rifle, the one she used to put the goat out of its misery, the day Grandeddy carelessly backed over it with his truck. My body was moving fast now. I counted my movements faster than I counted Deddy's. I cocked the rifle the way I saw Granmama do it. I pulled the trigger.

In the explosion everything—Deddy, Ella Mae, Grandeddy's house—disappeared, leaving only white light for a second, then smoke, then a dark calm. The porch light was gone, the crickets were silent, then a voice entered, it was Deddy's, "You stupid bitch!" Blood was pouring from between his fingers where he held his shoulder. He stood up to see where I was, where Ella Mae was, where his gun was. The rifle was still in my hands, and I cocked it again and held on tight even though my arms were trembling and numb. I knew I would never be able to fire a second shot. My eyes darted back and forth from Deddy to where I thought Ella Mae should be. Though he was bleeding, Deddy smirked at my trembling and took a step closer grimacing before smiling again.

"I see that bitch done taught you a thing or two about actin like you crazy, but you a fool, 'cause I think she done run off like a wounded animal and left you here to fend for yourself."

He reached down to pick up his belt, keeping his eyes on the quivering barrel of the rifle, my eyes at the other end meaning to aim again if it would save me.

He pulled a handkerchief from his pocket and used his teeth to help him strap the belt over the nicked shoulder. He looked satisfied to free up both hands, and before I could think, he snatched the rifle by the barrel end.

The moon rose up like a second sun in the darkness to the left of Grandeddy's porch. And there Ella Mae stood behind him, the light picking up the shiny sleekness of her hair. She held Deddy's gun to his head.

Her voice came shaky but strong. "Odessa, move on away now." I still could not see her eyes, but scurried to get up on the porch behind her. Her big hand was around the back of Deddy's neck now, and my heart beat in my throat.

Deddy was grimacing in pain but laughing, high-pitched like he did when he was drunk.

"I ain't got time to stand here and listen to your crazy ass. What the hell you supposed to be, a super fuckin hero? I don't give a damn what you do with Odessa. She right where she belongs, down here in the fuckin country. I ain't never wanted Bernice taking your bastard child back to St. Louis no way. Your half-Indian mama was crazy as you. Bernice should've let her bury 'Dessa out in the woods somewhere like her crazy ass was fixin to do."

Her hand went limp from Deddy's neck, but the gun was shaking now, the trigger loose against metal as it tapped Deddy's head—metal and skull bone, my teeth grinding against teeth.

Your bastard child—bury 'Dessa in the woods somewhere— bury 'Dessa in the woods somewhere—your bastard child.

My gritty hands made mud on my damp face, and I struggled to hold in the cry that escaped from my mouth, past my palms. It pealed out in the bare space around the house.

The sound of my cry was silenced by the shots; they rang out again and again and again, until his gun was empty. I had never stopped screaming. I opened my eyes.

Ella Mae held the gun over her head—wood chips and pieces of wasp nest fell from where she had mangled the porch ceiling. Her breath was so heavy, angry grunts, she screamed, "Leave! Leave! Leave!"

Deddy hurried to the van, trying to maintain some amount of cool in his step. When he stood safe in the door of the van, he had the last word, and I was glad that I could not see his eyes for what he said to me.

"You ain't been nothin but a fuckin pain in the ass. 'Dessa, I don't give a damn what you been told, you ain't my damn kid." Then he turned to Ella Mae, who was still holding the gun above her head. "Who Jim Dandy let fuck her up in them woods didn't have shit to do with me. Me and Bernice just tried to save your ass and give you somethin different than livin down here like a heathen. But I guess ain't a damn thing I can do to keep the truth a the matter from comin full circle.

"If either one of you ever round here when I come back down to bring my *real* kids to visit they grandeddy, I'm gonna try to shoot another hole in your ass."

My eyes receded into the place before there were glasses, before I watched Granmama's last walk up her porch steps, before I was born, and I was numb. He sped out using one arm to steer. The van careened in the path of its own light.

I remembered Granmama rocking me on that last night, singing.

> *I'm gonna fly away*
> *I'm gonna fly a-way.*

Kissing my sweaty cheeks that night.

> *To a land where*
> *To a land where*
> *Sickness will be no more.*

And the next day, I strained to see her through the dirty glass of the back window of that station wagon. I saw her climb the stairs, and she was gone, she was gone. Everything that was familiar fled with her. Rocks pinged on the bumper of the wagon. My mother, my father, my sisters and brothers—sticky hands, spankings on Sunday mornings, whispered secrets of things that were now mute.

I slumped down on the musty porch. I was lost. Everything had been cut loose from me.

I floated away in the path of the moonlight. Rain began to fall from the sky in big drops. Ella Mae sat on the step like the morning after we first met. The space between us was massive, I could feel the rhythm of her breathing, and I closed my eyes.

Her hand passed the ridge of my neck in an uncertain, almost touch, until finally her embrace surrounded my perishing body. The rain fell heavier now, but the revelations kept us still in that moment.

From her chest came a trapped breath. Her cry rose up from Granmama's porch in long guttural sighs. No words, but pain, love, loss, rising up loud and coming down quiet, moving like thunder over the terrain of her tongue and lips, a familiar comfort from someplace lost.

I let go of what held my limbs taut, and let her hold me. Her tears came like a warm stream salty in my mouth.

The two of us held each other tight, making a bridge over streams of our family's blood.

She muttered, "My baby . . . my baby."

About the Author

Zelda Lockhart's poetry, fiction, and essays have appeared in publications including *WordWrights, Sojourner, Calyx,* and *Sinister Wisdom.* She received her BA from Norfolk State University, and her MA in Literature from Old Dominion University.